TOMBSTONE TEN GAUGE

Another 30 yards and the rig turned sharply to the right, leaving Morgan 40 feet from the farm wagon. Morgan raced toward it, zigzagging and firing three times at the wagon, where traces of the blue smoke still hung in the nearly windless morning.

The bushwhacker wasn't moving.

Morgan moved over with his six-gun covering the man. He lifted the man's head from the wagon wheel and saw the blood on the side of it. The bushwhacker was dead.

Morgan looked around. Two men with guns drawn walked slowly toward him. He lowered his own revolver and frowned. Now he could see the men clearer and they both wore silver stars.

"Stand easy, stranger, and drop that six-gun. I'm the law in this town and I don't like to see our citizens shot down on the street in broad daylight."

BUCKSKIN #31

TOMBSTONE TEN GAUGE

KIT DALTON

LEISURE BOOKS NEW YORK CITY

A LEISURE BOOK®

October 2005

Published by

Dorchester Publishing Co., Inc.
200 Madison Avenue
New York, NY 10016

ISBN 0-8439-3182-5

TOMBSTONE TEN GAUGE

Chapter One

Thirty-five cowboys, miners, dayworkers, and store clerks looked up from their drinks in the Amigo Saloon in Santa Fe, New Mexico Territory, and gaped open-mouthed at the action playing out in front of them.

None of them had ever seen a man draw a hog-leg so fast. Buckskin Lee Morgan's hand whipped down and up in a fraction of a second, and before the other man had his six-gun out of leather the tall man in the black hat with red diamonds around the band had sent a .45 slug into the ceiling over his head, cocked the weapon, and centered the sights on the man's chest.

"Little friend, I ain't got no call to kill you, but unless you drop that iron back in your leather, you've got a date with the local undertaker in about ten seconds." The tall man with a square-cut face that was clean-shaven stared at the other gunman from clear brown and now deadly eyes.

The second man was shorter by half a foot at five-six. He wore trail clothes still showing the dust. He stared wide-eyed at the deadly black muzzle of Lee Morgan's Colt, and slowly relaxed his hand and pushed his own weapon back into the holster.

The haze of smoke from the one shot drifted slowly away from Morgan and he nodded at the other man.

"Finish your beer and get out of here, and thank your patron saint that you aren't a corpse by now. The next time you get mad and draw on a stranger it might just be your last gunfight."

Morgan watched the drifter as he finished the beer and stared with a little more bravado now at Morgan as he went by.

"I'll remember you, shooter. I never forget a face, or an insult." He walked on past. Morgan turned as he went, his big right hand hovering near his holster.

The barkeep grinned at Morgan and pushed a freshly drawn beer to him down the bar.

"Thanks, stranger. Been trying to get that little no-account out of the bar for three hours."

Morgan picked up the beer and drank half of it, then took a big breath and watched the apron.

"You been in town long?"

"Seven years next month."

"I'm looking for a young lady, might have worked here." Morgan took out a four-by-five-inch tintype photograph and showed it to the barkeep.

"Oh, yes, Miss Mitsy Maloy, least that's the name she used here. She was a dandy. Not used up like most of our girls. Know what I mean? She was bright and fresh. Course after a few months she did wear a little. Hard little lady to forget."

"Not here any more, then?"

"True. She moved on, oh, maybe five, six months ago. She told me she was heading for Albuquerque, then on over into Arizona—Phoenix, she figured, or maybe Flagstaff."

Buckskin Lee Morgan finished the beer. "Much obliged. Didn't like the look in that hombre's eyes when he left. I reckon he's got a Winchester rifle all aimed at your front door waiting for me to come out. You mind if I use the back door?"

"Not at all. But I was hoping that you'd put some hot lead in that little bastard's heart. He's been causing trouble hereabouts for a week now."

"Dead men have a way of slowing a man down. I'm heading south and then probably west. Thanks again for the beer."

A half hour later, Morgan rode out of a livery stable at the edge of Santa Fe on the back of a big, thick-chested buckskin he had just bought. He had bounced for four days down the road from Denver in one damned hard seat after another in that Celerity wagon. He was still bruised and sore and dead sick of riding a stage.

Albuquerque coming up. If the girl wasn't there he'd consider taking a stage on to Flagstaff. That was a long ride. He had 60 miles to think about it.

This job had started in Denver, two weeks ago. He had seen an ad in the *Rocky Mountain News* for a "tracker, detective, and a man good with a gun." Since Morgan was broke at the time, and qualified, he'd answered the ad.

The man's name was Hans Roustenhauser, a German immigrant who had made a fortune brewing and selling a new German-type beer in Denver. He lived in a big house in the Heights, and had three servants that Morgan saw and probably half a dozen more.

The man was in his sixties, dressed well, but had a haunted look to him. There evidently was no Mrs. Roustenhauser. He was about five-nine, heavy-built, partly bald through graying hair, with thick muttonchop sideburns and a full mustache. He nodded quickly after he listened to some of Morgan's background. Then he took him outside and had him draw and shoot at a bottle in the back of the large back garden.

Morgan hit the bottle the first time from 30 feet in a fast draw he had been practicing on. His usually fast draw was honed to a fine edge, and the brewmaster was impressed.

Back upstairs in an expensively furnished den, Roustenhauser told Morgan he was hired.

"A handshake is the only contract we need," Roustenhauser said. "My word is as good as gold." He produced a tintype photograph and showed it to Morgan.

"This is my daughter, Hortense. She's a little over twenty-three years old. She's been missing from her home now for just over three years. She hates Denver. Her favorite place was Santa Fe. I expect she went there, but I have heard that she is not there now. I can't give you any dates."

"You want me to find her?" Morgan asked. He adjusted the weapon on his thigh.

"Yes, find her and bring her back here to Denver."

"Not a chance, Mr. Roustenhauser. She's of age. This is a free country. Hortense can go anywhere she wants to. I'd be guilty of kidnapping if I brought her back here against her will."

"Now just a minute!" the German said, his voice rising.

Morgan's hand flexed over the weapon and the

thickset man saw the motion. He stopped.

"First, I don't like being shouted at," Morgan said evenly but with a bite of steel in the tone. "Second, I'll find the girl, but whether she comes back or not is up to her. If she wants to come back, I'll escort her back here. That's the best I can promise."

The German brewmaster and successful brewery owner sat down heavily in a large chair. The anger had faded from his face. Now he was simply a father who had lost his child. He looked up, an expression of hope and pleading.

"Can you find her?"

"With this picture, there's a good chance. She's a beautiful young lady. That will be a help to me."

"I'll pay you well."

"I'll need my expenses. There probably will be a lot of travel by horse and stage, maybe even train if she went east. My expenses and five dollars a day."

Roustenhauser looked up quickly. "So much?"

Morgan knew he had surprised the brewmaster. The average working man made $30 a month in wages, or a little over a dollar a day. He figured he was worth five times that.

"How much is your daughter worth to you, Mr. Roustenhauser? That's my price. If you don't hire me, I'll get another job. It's not that important to me."

The brewery owner sighed, nodded. "Ya, goot. I will do it. I will give you five hundred dollars expense money now. Wire me if you need more money. When you find her I will pay you five dollars for each day it takes."

"What else can you tell me about her? Her height, approximate weight, color of hair, eyes, the usual description."

"Ya. My Hortense is five feet three. She has blue eyes and blonde hair. She has a scar on her right arm below the elbow on back where she fell and cut herself on a glass she carried. What else?"

"That should do nicely, Mr. Roustenhauser. The picture will be a big help. Do you have the expense money here?"

The brewmaster nodded. "She must come home. She's the only child I have. My wife is gone. I need some family here. Everyone else is back . . . in Germany."

He opened a drawer, made some movements which Morgan decided were those of dialing a combination safe. A few moments later he brought out federal bank notes.

"Will greenbacks be all right?"

"Some places discount the greenbacks by thirty per cent. Better make half of that in gold double eagles."

Roustenhauser counted out the money.

That afternoon Morgan checked the stage routes and schedules. There was a stage line that had one Celerity rig heading south every second day. It would be going again tomorrow. He bought a ticket, and had one more night on the town before he left for Santa Fe.

Morgan broke out of the reverie and concentrated on the stage road. Hard for a man to get lost going south to Albuquerque along here.

It took him two days, since he didn't push, and he arrived in the town thirsty, dirty, and wanting a bed and bath even more than a good meal. He had ridden a little harder that second day, and got into town just before dusk, stabled his buckskin, and taken a room at the New Mexico Inn, a two-story hotel that boasted 24 rooms.

After his bath it took him to midnight to find anyone who remembered the girl.

"Hell, yes, I remember her. Fancy little woman, acted all prissy and uppity like she was a great lady. The guys around here loved it. She was busier than any two other whores in town. I was one of her best customers. But hell, she left here six months ago. Said she was going to Tombstone because she'd heard how that was the wildest town in the world. I made her promise to carry a derringer with her down there, all the damn time."

It took Morgan five more days on the stage, a big Concord this time with six horses out front, to get to Flagstaff, to Phoenix, and on down to Tombstone, half a rifle shot from the Mexican border.

Already the place was rich from silver mines. Used to be the only people living in the barren high dry country were cattle ranchers along the San Pedro River. Cattlemen were there before the town sprang up. The cowboys used to drive their cattle, some raised and many rustled from across the border, up to the San Carlos Indian reservation and sell them to the government to feed the Indians. When the town of Tombstone built up, the cattlemen had a good-sized beef market right next door.

But silver was king, and gambling, whoring, and drinking were the three princes that kept the 27 saloons roaring, many of them 24 hours a day.

Buckskin Lee Morgan did not take to travel with good humor. He'd rather rustle a pack of three-foot rattlers. Now that he'd made it there, he took a hotel room in the best-looking hostelry he could find, and then had a real meal with a cloth on the table and silverware.

It was almost noon when he began his survey. A bath, a clean shirt, and a brushed-off black jacket and string tie helped mark him as a man of some means. The first three barkeeps hardly looked at the picture, just shook their heads and went back to serving beer and shots of watered-down whiskey.

The fourth apron nodded. "Damn, figured she was too good to be true first time I saw her. Yeah, she's in town. Don't know what name you have, but around here she's known as Miss Lily Larue. Used to be just a dance hall girl until she won the big poker game. She used to play a lot of poker and usually won. Then one night she took on the big boys with four thousand dollars tucked into her bosom and wiped out three of them, then bested the Sutherland brothers and won their saloon, the Silver Queen."

Morgan dropped a dime on the bar and took a draft beer in a big glass mug. "She still own the saloon?"

"Indeed she does. Moved up into management, might say. She don't do no whoring no more."

"How old would you guess this Miss Lily is?"

"Old? Damn, I'm no good with painted women. Between eighteen and thirty somewhere, young-ish."

Morgan nodded his thanks and finished the beer. He drifted out of the saloon and saw the sign for the Silver Queen halfway down the block.

Morgan walked in the door and saw that this place was a cut above the other saloons he'd seen in town. It had a long mirror behind the bar, brass rail, tables where house dealers handled the gambling chores, and a stairway up one side of the open area to a second floor for the whores.

He saw the cashier where chips were for sale, and bought $40 worth and found a chair open at a dollar-limit table. Morgan played for a half hour, watching everything around him. He didn't concentrate on the cards, but even so won $20. He moved to a ten-dollar-limit game and quickly won $100, then dropped $20 and won another pot with more than $120 in it.

"Seems to be your lucky night, cowboy."

The woman's voice came from behind his chair, and now he caught the scent of perfume, not the heavy kind the whores wore, but something faint and interesting and expensive.

"Just a game of cards, ma'am," he said, not turning. It was his deal. He made it five-card draw, jacks or better to open, and kept his cards close to his chest. He had a pair of queens and three low cards. The second man around the table opened and Morgan relaxed without any outward sign.

There were six players and the ante had been five dollars. The opener made it ten to stay. There was $90 in the pot. More watchers moved toward the table. Two players took two cards, one took one card, and the other three wanted three draw cards —Morgan took three.

Two men dropped out. Evidently they couldn't beat the openers. The man who opened bet ten, another man raised him five, and it came $15 to Morgan. He bumped it to $20 and the opener upped it another ten. Morgan was the last man to call or raise. He called. There were $210 in the pot.

The opener showed his cards. Aces and jacks. Morgan had checked his cards right after the deal, but held them so close no one else could see them. Two of the men threw in their hands, and that left Morgan and the opener.

"Aces and jacks, nice hand, but mine is better, a trio of queens." Morgan spread out his cards on the table. The man who had opened shrugged, and counted the chips left in front of him as Morgan reached out and pulled in the big-money pot. Some men worked all year for $210.

Someone tapped him on the shoulder. He looked around.

The lady with the subtle perfume was not a dance

hall girl, at least not dressed in the showy, flashy way they usually did. She was a blonde with sharp blue eyes—about five-three, he figured—and she had a commanding way about her.

"Mister, I want to see you for a minute. I'm sure the boys here won't mind you sitting out a hand or two. Right over here at my table."

Morgan stared at her a minute. "Miss, you realize you're breaking my run of luck. A lady just doesn't do that sort of thing."

"I'm no lady," she said, and turned and walked over to a table near the back of the room that had a fancy tablecloth on it, two candles lit, and delicate, expensive chairs with cushions. She stood there waiting for him, tapping one small foot in expensive black pumps.

Morgan looked at the other men around the table, pocketed the stack of chips, and shrugged.

"I better see what the lady wants." The men nodded and watched him with new interest.

"Yeah, Miss Lily don't like to be kept waiting."

"Save my chair," Morgan said, tipping it so the back rested against the poker table. Then he walked over to the woman who still tapped her foot.

"Took you damn long enough."

"I don't cotton to orders by people I don't know. Who are you and what do you want?"

She grinned and sat down. "Yeah, good, I like a little fire in a man. My name is Miss Lily Larue, and there are two men I want you to kill."

Chapter Two

Morgan looked at her closely. This had to be Hortense Roustenhauser, now known as Miss Lily Larue, owner of the Silver Queen pleasure palace.

"What was that, miss?"

"I said I have two men I want you to kill."

"You've got the wrong man."

"I don't think so. Not the way you walk, the way you play poker, the way you have that well-worn Colt .45 tied down to your thigh. You know what to do with a six-gun, no doubt. I've seen three or four men like you before. Not a lot, there aren't many who can do the job. You can."

She sat down and signaled to the bar. A moment later the barkeep came with two mugs of beer.

"Cold artesian well water. Best I can do in place of ice. But it cools down a beer mighty nice. I keep

cold well water circulating around my keg of beer."
She pushed one beer over in front of the other chair.

"Don't be impolite, sit down and let's talk. My
name is Lily Larue." She held out her hand. He
shook it, then sat down.

"Great name you picked out. I don't have much
time to find a new name, so you can call me Lee
Morgan." He tipped the beer. It was cold. He hadn't
had any cold beer since he left the high country.

"Morgan? Is that your real name?" He nodded.
She grinned. "Yes, I think I'm going to like you, Lee
Morgan. The man can shoot and he has a sense of
humor. You probably leave your victims laughing."

"True, some have laughed themselves to death."

"Which brings us back to business. I have a small
job for you."

"I'm not an executioner. I told you that you have
the wrong man."

"I still don't think so. You may know that a few
months ago, about six by now, I won this saloon and
pleasure palace in a poker game. A high-stakes
game. I went in with four thousand dollars and
promptly lost the first three hands. Then I bet my
last dollar on a pot and won it.

"After that I won ten pots in a row and I didn't
cheat. On the last hand, I bet twenty thousand
dollars, which was that much more cash than the
Sutherland brothers had. They thought they had me
beaten with three kings so they threw a signed grant
deed for the Silver Queen into the pot to cover the
twenty thousand. It wasn't and isn't worth that
much, but I let it stand.

"They called me and I lay down four sevens.
Roscoe Sutherland, who was playing the hand,
dropped his cards in a panic. There were fifty
witnesses. I owned the saloon all legal and proper.
They didn't take it gracefully. For the past two

months the Sutherland brothers have been threatening to sue me to get their property back. I laugh at them.

"Last night they came in and shot up the place. I had them arrested, but they're out of jail now awaiting a trial. They swear they'll kill me and take back their saloon."

"Will they?"

"Try to kill me? Yes."

"I've been known to hire out as a bodyguard."

"How much?"

"Three dollars a day."

"You're hired."

"Sawed-off shotgun?"

"Behind the bar, two of them."

"Double-ought buck?"

"Wally can help you. Come on over."

He took the cold beer with him. The introductions were made. Wally was thick of body with massive hairy arms. He had one eye that drooped from a knife-fight cut, and a big friendly grin. He handed Morgan a sawed-off Greener. The barrels were less than a foot long.

"I always keep buckshot on the right, double-ought on the left in these side-by-siders," Wally said.

"Good plan, but I want both double-buck and six extra rounds," Morgan told him. They made the changes and Morgan pocketed the extra rounds. He held the weapon against his leg as he walked back toward the table where they had been sitting. He was looking for a good stash spot where the Greener would be handy yet out of sight.

He found it on the back wall under some window drapes that covered not a window but just a chunk of the wall. They were a woman's touch in the man's domain. He slid the Greener behind the drape at floor level and it was out of sight. He stood it with the stock and butt plate upward so he could grab it and bring it up to fire in one swift move.

Back at Lily's table, he sat down and finished the beer. "What do these Sutherland jaspers look like?" he asked.

"Both are small, about five-four, and slender. They always wear identical black suits, vests, white shirts, gold pocket watches with gold chains and gold fobs. Never see them without their black derby hats."

"Sidearms?"

"Both wear six-guns, and I'd guess each one has at least one hideout, probably two-shot derringers."

"They kill as dead as a Sharps Big Fifty."

"Where you staying in town?"

"Hanover House."

"Best in town. If you don't mind sleeping in a whorehouse, we got a guard's room downstairs in back you're welcome to use. Then too, we set a good table."

"I best stay at the hotel. You open all night?"

"No, I don't have enough people. Not much going on from two in the morning until noon the next day. Them's our off hours. I want you here from noon to two A.M."

"Reckon I can do that. You know, Tombstone reminds me a lot of a street somewhere. Where is it? The gambling halls and bawdy house street. Yeah, Tryton Street in Denver. Reminds me of that hell-hole."

He watched her, but she didn't react in surprise or alarm.

"You've been to Denver?" she asked.

"Sure, everybody's been to Denver. You too?"

"Passed through once. Didn't like it. Oh, no gambling while you're working. You'll get too inter-ested in your game. I don't have a whit of an idea when the Sutherlands might come. You can take care of drunks too, and the moochers. We have some steadies I let stay, I'll tell you which ones. But never more than two of them at the same time."

"I better cash in these chips and start earning my pay," Morgan said. He went to the cashier and came away with $245 in gold.

As he waited for the chips to be counted, he considered his next move. He had found the girl, but what the hell did he do now? He couldn't send a telegram to Roustenhauser that his daughter was a whore, a madam, and a saloon owner in Tombstone, Arizona Territory. The old German would shoot himself.

As he tracked the girl, he had sent a wire each time he had found out something new, and by now the brewmaster knew he was heading for Tombstone. Morgan knew he needed to have a heart-to-heart talk with Miss Lily/Hortense, but not right away.

His other big problem was thinking about that wanted poster on him. He had flinched when the man said Hortense was coming to Tombstone. It had been four years ago and the town had just been starting when he had the small, deadly problem here that had put his face on a wanted poster.

It was the Arizonian Saloon and the young man had been drunk. He fell against Morgan and pushed him in anger. A moment later the same young man fell across Morgan's poker table breaking it to the floor and ruining the game. The young man came up dazed, furious and swinging. He hit Morgan.

He could only half see, and missed Morgan twice then with roundhouse swings. He scowled, bellowed in rage, took a gunslinger's stance, and demanded that Morgan shoot it out with him right there, right then.

The drinkers and card players scattered away from the two and out of the way of any line of fire. Morgan tried to talk the kid out of it, but the young man was too blind drunk to listen to any reason. Two of his friends came and dragged him away, but a minute later he was back, swearing at Morgan, calling him every dirty name he could think of.

Morgan told the kid to go home and sleep it off. Instead the twenty-year-old whirled with his gun out and shot into the floor near Morgan. Then he jammed his gun back into his holster.

"Now, damn you, bastard, we'll shoot it out. Right here. You better draw because I'm going to and you'll be supper tonight for some buzzard."

They were about 20 feet apart.

"Don't do it, kid," Morgan said. "I have no reason to kill you."

"Damn right you do. You don't kill me, I'm gonna kill you."

They stared at each other for a minute. The saloon was cleared behind them and between them with 20 men huddled against the far wall.

Then the kid started to draw. He was agonizingly slow. Morgan waited for him, then drew and shot him in the right shoulder, his gun side. The young man's weapon wasn't out of leather yet.

The 140-pound man spun around and slammed three feet to the rear and crashed to the floor. He screamed and turned around in the sawdust as he lifted his six-gun.

"Drop it, kid!" Morgan shouted.

The youngster fired, and missed by three feet. He fired again, and missed on the other side.

Morgan shot him in the left shoulder.

"Give it up, kid, and stay alive," Morgan called again.

This time the kid's six-gun aimed better and

Morgan fired quickly before the other man could pull the trigger. The round caught the youth under the chin and tore half of the top of his head off when it came out. There was no reason to check to see if he was still alive.

The Tombstone city police chief rushed in a moment later. He saw the situation. He took statements from four men who had seen it all. Then talked to Morgan.

"Seems to be a case of self-defense, Morgan," the chief said. "They say you told him three or four times to drop his gun. He started the trouble, he called you out. Everyone says so. You come by the office with me and I'll have you sign a paper to this effect and you won't be held."

Morgan thanked him. "His doing entirely, Chief. Who was he anyway?"

"There we might have a problem. He's the younger brother of the county sheriff. I have jurisdiction in the city limits, but Sheriff Potts handles the rest of Cochise County. We don't always see eye to eye on law enforcement. This is my jurisdiction, but he sometimes comes on hard, and with the kid being his younger brother and all—might be a good idea if you moved on out of town before Sheriff Potts gets back from the territorial capital."

Morgan had no more business in Tombstone and rode out that afternoon, and thought that was the end of it. He was in Phoenix a month later when he saw the wanted poster tacked to a wall. He remembered the words well, and had seen them often during the past four years. The poster said:

"Wanted for Murder . . . Dead or Alive . . . Buckskin Lee Morgan. Reward $2,000 for the shooting death of Wilfred Potts. Contact Tombstone Sheriff, Tombstone, Arizona Territory."

The $2,000 reward was six years' pay for the

average worker or cowhand. It had sent dozens of quick-money bounty hunters on Lee Morgan's trail, and had caused him a lot of problems and a few gunshot wounds in the past.

He had come back to Tombstone knowing he faced that old danger here, but determined as well to get the problem cleared up once and for all. It was not a legal wanted poster. The sheriff must know that. What he had to find out was who was the sheriff now. Had to see if the old sheriff, Latimore Potts, was still in town, and just what the chief of police would have to say about the whole matter.

It was touchy, but nothing that he shouldn't be able to take care of while he was in town. At least it seemed that way.

Morgan took the big mug of beer and went back to the table he had picked out to the rear of the 40-foot-long hall. It was within reach of the drapery and the shotgun, and he would have his back firmly against the wall. He had an ideal view of the place. If it got crowded he could stand up and see everyone there.

Lady Lily came past and watched him. "This going to be your roost?"

"One of them."

"Looks like a good one. Oh, have a beer or two when you want one, on the house. Just be sure you can do your job—damn, I shouldn't have said that. I know you'll do the job. With the girls upstairs, it's different. You don't look like the kind of man who has to pay for love, but if you go upstairs for it, you pay for it."

"Sounds fair. Any of your regular moochers in here now?"

"Just one—Old Bill. Guy must be seventy-five and drinks anything he can grab. Until I caught on, he'd come in yelling that there was a shoot-out in the street. Three or four guys would charge outside leaving their beer and he'd grab them and drain them in a few gulps and sneak out the back door. Got me a willow switch and talked him out of that one.''

Old Bill was bent and twisted, with a full beard and bleary eyes. He stood at the bar beside a man who was talking to someone else. The drinker turned away to shout at a man down the bar and Old Bill grabbed his mug of beer and drained it, then slid it back in place.

Lady Lily shook her head and went up to the bar, showed the man his empty glass, and asked the barkeep to give him another one to replace it.

That seemed to set the tone for the Silver Queen. It was a better-class saloon than most, and Lily seemed to have a calming influence on the men.

Now if he could talk to the sheriff with the same degree of calm and reasonable communication, he might be able to settle this illegal wanted poster for good. If . . . He knew that was a hell of a big if.

Chapter Three

A little after ten o'clock that evening the two short Sutherland brothers marched into the Silver Queen. Two big toughs strode right behind them. All four were wearing six-guns.

Morgan grabbed the Greener and held it at his side as he moved through the tables toward the four men.

One of the brothers turned toward the barkeep. "You're out of a job, Wally, as of now. Take off your apron and git."

Wally stared at him a moment, then started to nod and dropped out of sight behind the bar.

Nate Sutherland drew his six-gun and swore. He started around the end of the bar when Morgan's voice, tipped with steel authority, stopped him.

"Take another step, Sutherland, and you're dead."

Nate looked up at the twin barrels of the Greener.

"Don't worry, I've got the other three covered with the other barrel. You want to get your insides blown all over this saloon or not?"

Slowly Nate lowered the six-gun and pushed it into leather.

"You're a damn poor poker player, Sutherland. Now you just made another stupid draw against a pat hand. Why don't you cut your losses right now before you die? Turn around and take your trained elephants and your kin and get out of this saloon. The next time you step through the door, you're going to get blown right back to the street with a load of double-ought buck. You understand the new rules around here?"

Nate nodded, turned slowly, his eyes wide, the surprise and anger still showing on his face. He walked slowly to the other three, motioned with his hand, and they turned as well and went out the front door.

Morgan moved like a cougar to the front opening and watched through it a moment, then eased outside. The four men stood 20 feet down the street talking.

The Greener pointed well over their heads at the sky, Morgan pulled the trigger once. The shotgun blast sent all four men rushing down the street in panic. Forty yards away, they stopped and stared back at Morgan.

"I won't forget this, whoever you are," Nate snarled. "You're a dead man, you just don't know it yet."

"Anytime, runt. But you better bring a better army than you have now." Morgan could barely see the small men in light that splashed from a nearby saloon. He could tell that the brothers were furious as they vanished into the nearby drinking emporium.

Morgan turned and found Miss Lily three feet behind him.

"You do good work, Morgan." She put her hand through his arm and led him back inside. "Wally is your friend for life. He used to work for Sutherland. You probably just saved my saloon from being turned into a trash dump. New rules. You want to go upstairs, you get a free pass anytime."

"Just doing my job."

Inside, several of the patrons clapped when they saw Morgan.

"Them little bastards been running this town long enough," one man said, lifting his beer. He went to the bar and brought Morgan a fresh tap brew and thanked him again.

Morgan nodded at the people, opened the Greener and took out the spent round, and pushed in a new one. That quieted the gamblers and drinkers. He walked back to his table and Miss Lily went with him.

She sat down and then he sat and looked at her. She was as beautiful as her picture. Eyes that hid nothing—whatever she thought showed in her soft blues. Skin like a peach, unblemished. A regal nose, dainty and firm, over a small mouth that seemed to hold a smile most of the time.

"You're staring at me," she said.

"True. A beautiful woman must get used to being stared at."

"Thanks, but I'm not in the business anymore."

"I know, I'm looking for a favor. What do you know about the chief of police?"

"He's new. Been on the job about six months. Seems to be honest and does a good job. He might be taking a dollar or two to check doors at night, but he doesn't get a big salary."

"Sounds good to me. I've got a small problem here in town I'd like to tell you about. You have a few minutes?"

"I knew you were too good to be true. I finally get a man who has the backbone to stand up to the Sutherlands and now I find out that he has a problem."

"Not a big problem, and don't worry, the Sutherlands will be dealt with." He told her about the wanted poster and how it came about. When he was finished she took a big breath.

"Is that all? Doesn't sound like much of a problem to me. Your friend, Latimore Potts, the former sheriff, is now a big gun up in Phoenix in the Territorial Legislature. At least he *thinks* he's a real cannon. He doesn't have much power here in town anymore. The current county sheriff is Edgar Dirkin. He was handpicked by Potts when he ran for the legislature. Dirkin has been in office for four years or so. He's strictly a Potts man on everything. He owes his soul to Potts."

"I was hoping. . . ."

"It should be all right with the police chief. His name is John Inman. He's a fair-minded man."

"Tomorrow, could you go see him? Say you saw a man in your place you thought was on a wanted poster and look through the ones he has? I want to know if there's that old wanted on me still in his files."

"Easy, but I'll do it right now. I know the night man over at the city jail. He'll show me the stack of wanteds."

"Good. I'll keep the rabble under control here."

When Miss Lily left, Morgan settled down with a fresh beer and watched the crowd. He hadn't paid much attention to the girls. There were six or eight of them and most of them stayed busy upstairs. When they had a slow time, they came down and sold drinks to the men as they looked for business.

One of them came over and sat down at Morgan's table. She was small and dark, some Spanish blood in her background. She had on a dance hall dress, tight at the waist, and cut low to show off half of her pushed-up breasts.

He could see a line of sweat on her forehead. She grinned at him. "Hear you're our new hired gun."

"New?" Morgan asked. "There have been others?"

"One or two. They never stayed long. Want to go upstairs for a poke? Lady Lily tells us it's no charge to you."

"I'm working," he said.

She pouted. "That means you're too high and mighty to poke a whore, right?"

"Depends on the woman."

"You don't have to be delicate. I'm a whore, a fucking whore. I'm not sensitive about the word."

"Neither am I. A woman is whatever she thinks she is. Most of the whores I have known have been mighty decent women down on their luck. I don't judge. I don't throw stones. I bet you'd be great in bed. But like I say, I'm working." He saw two men arguing at the bar. "Excuse me, a small duty to perform."

Morgan was almost there when one of the two men clubbed the other one with a hard right fist.

"Hold it!" Morgan barked. Both men turned and looked at him. "New policy in the Silver Queen, gents. You want to fight with your fists, you each put up a fifty-dollar deposit. Then if you don't smash up anything or cause any damage, you get the fifty dollars back."

"Don't have no fifty dollars. That's two months' pay!" The larger man bellowed it out in anger.

"Then you can't fight inside. Fistfighting is good for a man, sharpens him up. But you'll have to take it outside."

The two men glared at each other, then the smaller one shrugged. "The hell with it," he said, and walked away. The other fighter snorted and turned back to his beer at the bar.

Wally grinned at Morgan. "Wish all of them were that easy," he said.

"Me too," Morgan agreed, and went back to his table. The small dark girl had left. He saw her leading a man up the stairs.

Ten minutes later, Miss Lily was back.

"I talked with the new officer. He said the chief told him that he only kept wanted posters for a year, then he threw out the old ones. Yours wasn't among the ones he has in his wanted drawer."

"Good. I appreciate. That leaves the sheriff."

"I'll go around there in the morning before opening time. I've never had any trouble with Dirkin." Lily looked up at him. "You going to be safe tonight? I didn't like the way the Sutherlands looked at you."

"Safe? I haven't been safe for eight years. Man learns to live with a bit of danger. Spices up things a bit."

"But you wouldn't mind a suggestion?"

"Not at all."

"Stay away from the Bird Cage Saloon. I hear the Sutherlands have made that their unofficial headquarters lately. They have a lot of friends there."

"Isn't that where they have the wild entertainers?"

"Some say. The girls almost do on stage what mine do for two dollars a throw upstairs in private."

"But not quite do it."

"True." She watched him. "Now, I have one more suggestion. After we close up at two A.M., there's no sense your walking all the way down to your hotel. You can stay here tonight."

He looked up at her.

She sucked in a little breath and watched him closely. "Stay in my room."

He hesitated and she looked away. "I know, you don't have to. I told you I'm not in that business anymore, I'm management." She took a couple of quick little gasps and he thought she was going to cry.

"Hey, no, not that at all. I don't judge people. Anyway, that doesn't matter at all to me." He nodded. "Oh, yes, Miss Lily, I'd just love to stay here tonight."

She smiled. "Good, it's almost midnight. You make sure that Wally locks the front door and let him out the back and then bar both. I'm going to go up to my room and straighten it up a little." She grinned. "Also, I'm going to have a bath. Go to the head of the stairs, then turn right, the last door in the hall."

"I bet I can find it."

Morgan watched the drinkers and gamblers the rest of the night and nothing outrageous happened. He broke up one small fight, tossed out two panhandlers who were bothering the customers, and helped flush everyone out of the place at two o'clock in the morning.

"You lock up?" Morgan asked Wally.

He nodded. "All except the back door. I need to go out, and then you can lock it and put in the big bar across the door."

Five minutes later Morgan walked up the stairs and heard one or two of the girls still working. They had to let their customers out themselves.

The last door on the right had a sign on it that said: "Private. No Admittance. That means you, Buster!" He knocked on the door and it came open at once.

"Good, you came," Miss Lily said. She wore a sleek, tight red dress that swept the floor, and outlined every curve of her beautiful body on the way down. The bodice was low and showed off more than half of each breast.

"Beautiful!" he said. She had fixed her hair, the blonde locks cascading down her back held with a soft red ribbon that matched the dress.

"I think I'll let you come in. How do you like what the girls call my tigress lair?"

The whole room was done in pink. The wallpaper, the ceiling, the curtains. The bedstead had been painted pink, and a showy pink bedspread covered it right up to a dozen pillows of a darker shade of pink that showered down on the bed. To the far side sat a small working desk with shelves behind glass doors on the top. A secretary, some called it. It was in deep walnut tones.

"The whole place is remarkable. Who decorated it for you?"

"I did. The mail order catalog people and I are best friends."

He stepped inside and she closed the door.

Miss Lily smiled and pointed out to the hall. "I can just hear the girls out there tittering and giggling. They know that tomorrow will be hell on wheels, or an easy day, depending on what happens here tonight."

Morgan smiled. "Just what do you want to happen, Miss Lily?"

She looked at him and she was a thousand years old with the wisdom of the universe. "Sometimes, even a whore likes to be loved."

Chapter Four

Morgan watched the beautiful woman. "Lily, everyone wants to be loved. Sometimes the people themselves help make it hard. What about your parents? They must love you."

She turned away, the vulnerability in her face and attitude gone in an instant.

"My mother is dead and I never speak of my father."

"I'm sorry. My parents are gone too." She led him to a softly pink patterned sofa against one wall. Lily sat at one end watching him.

"You know I don't want simply to have sex. That's too cold, too easy, too meaningless. I want something more."

"What is it? What do you want that I can give you?"

"I want you to hold me all night. I want you to tell me that I'm good and solid and worthwhile and not just another whore. I want you to look at me and see something besides a body you can relieve yourself in. I want you to smile with me, to laugh with me, to cry with me, to be with me whenever I need you and whenever you need me."

"You're talking about a lifetime of trusting and honoring and loving," Morgan said.

"I know. That's what I want from you. Why not you? You're strong and young and vital and from what I can see honest and trustworthy."

"You know nothing about me, Lily. I know nothing about you."

"Then *let's pretend*! Let's just imagine that we are deeply in love and that we honor and trust each other, that we do kind and gentle things for each other, and at night, when we go to bed, we respond to each other's basic physical needs."

"I'll try," he said.

Lily moved closer to him, reached out, and touched his cheek and then the square slant of his jaw.

"Such a beautiful face, so strong!"

She moved her hand and nodded to him. It was his turn.

Morgan reached out and traced the line of her chin down to her neck, then touched her nose.

"Beauty is at its best when it is beholden, beauty is reason enough in itself for being, beauty is amazing and so wondrous to find, it must be captured in an instant—or it is gone forever."

"You're a poet! That was marvelous." She closed her eyes, and her hands touched his face gently as though she were blind, then his hair and down his back, and by instinct her face came toward his, and without opening her eyes, she kissed his lips lightly, then came away.

He moved toward her until their thighs touched and he could feel the heat of her. He touched her shoulders and then her neck and the very tops of her breasts. Then he bent and kissed each white swell of flesh.

"Some poet said that woman is a mystery, a vaunted miracle, a brazen beauty, a wondrous wanton, a wife, and mother so tender, all wrapped in love and longing and forever . . . mystery."

Lily sighed and leaned toward him. Her eyes were closed and she lay her head on his shoulder. "I haven't heard such wonderful words since I left . . . left home. There was a poet I knew—a young poet who was the very first to make love to me. He was so soft and tender, so shy and unsure, so fumbling with his hands and his body—but so facile and sharp and smart in his mind. I found him totally fascinating. We made love that first time, and he told me it was the very first for him as well. Marvelous, so delicate, so gentle, so inquiring, so curious."

She leaned back and looked up at him. "Would you like to kiss me?"

He bent and brushed his lips tenderly across hers, then came back and kissed her again with more contact. The third time he kissed her his mouth was open, and he heard her gasp in delight and then opened her mouth.

A gentle moan came from deep in her throat. Her eyes blinked open for a moment, then drifted closed and she sighed. When the kiss ended she turned so her breasts pressed firmly against his chest. Her arms came around him and she pressed her head against his shoulder.

"So tender!" she whispered. "I can't really remember tenderness. It's been so long. So gentle and tender, so poetic. I always had to help Hartley. He was a poet, a scholar without a job, without any prospects. My father had him thrown out of the house. I left the same night. Hartley had nowhere to go, and now neither did I. I sold the jewelry I had brought with me. Two diamond rings and a fine ruby. Oh, damn!''

She reached up and kissed his cheek. "I won't speak of him again. You are just as tender, as understanding.''

Lily reached up and began to undo his shirt. The string tie went first, and then the buttons, and she stopped and pushed her hands inside his shirt and felt his chest and twined some of the blondish brown hair there.

She slid off his jacket, then the shirt, and when he was bare to the waist, she lifted his hands to her breasts. He found the buttons under a false panel and undid them down to her waist. She pushed the dress off her shoulders and let it fall. Only a soft cotton wrap bound her breasts so they would push up. She undid it quickly and then smiled at him.

Her breasts were not large, but fit the rest of her size. The areolas were faint and the nipples small and pink. He caught one breast with his hand and caressed it as if it were a precious jewel. Slowly he massaged and petted it and worked around and around until he came to the top.

Lily gasped gently as he rolled her nipple between his finger and thumb. Then he bent and kissed the swell of her mound. She had no reaction. He kissed her nipple and licked it gently with his tongue. Slowly it began to lift and rise and fill with blood. He nibbled at it, then bit it until she gasped in near-pain. He worked the other breast the same way, and when both of her nipples were pulsating, he kissed her lips again, the feather touch, the teasing kiss that was a promise unfulfilled.

"Oh, my," Lily said. "Oh, my!" Lily opened her eyes and stared at him. "Who are you, Lee Morgan, and why have you come here to bedevil me?"

He kissed her lips again, harder this time, then eased away. "Lily, I am here to love you."

She cried then, softly, but they were tears of joy and she smiled through them. In a moment the tears were gone, and she slid out of her skirt and petticoats and the flimsy cotton underwear and stood before him naked.

He marveled at the perfect body. Long, slender legs, beautifully formed, lean and exciting and strong with the softest, whitest inner thighs he had ever seen. The muff of blonde hair at her crotch was in more of a long line than a triangle, and it tried but could hide nothing.

She moved and her legs parted, and he saw the softly red nether lips of her treasure, so swollen and moist and ready. His glance moved higher to hips that flared just enough before her soft white flesh nipped in to a tiny waist above a softly curved belly.

Above her sleek and slender waist her rib cage came curving sharply up to her proud and thrown-out breasts.

"A masterpiece of sculpturing," Morgan said softly.

She came to him and led him to bed, and lay down curling almost into a ball.

"Will you love me tonight by holding me, by being here, by protecting me and honoring me, caressing me, enduring me without the promise of using my body—only to comfort me?"

"Of course, without question. But with a man's

hope for another day, another night when I can honor you with my own kind of loving."

"Done," she said, and motioned him to the bed. She undressed him, saw, surprisingly, that he had no erection, and smiled a soft, deep, secret smile as she lay down naked beside him on the bed and drew a light pink patterned sheet over them and snuggled close to him, kissing his shoulder, then his chest, and relaxing as she had done only once or twice in her lifetime.

Miss Lily Larue sighed contentedly. This was to be a night to remember, a night not like any other in her entire life. She smiled, watched him looking at her, then smiled gently and drifted off to sleep.

He awoke much later, felt her beside him, then opened his eyes and realized they hadn't turned down the lamp. She had one hand across his chest, the other cupping his genitals. He stretched over to the lamp and blew it out, then let the darkness settle over them like a blanket, enveloping them in its warmth and concern with a gentle, satisfying sense of caring for this lost young beauty.

He awoke when something tickled his nose. Morgan tried to brush it away, but it came back. He stirred, then opened one eye and in the daylight saw the woman sitting beside him on the bed. She was radiant, and smiled now impishly as she tickled his nose with her finger.

"Sleepyhead," she said softly. She bent and kissed his cheek, then turned his face and kissed his lips, but came away quickly.

"We don't eat breakfast here until noon, Buckskin Lee Morgan. If you want breakfast you'll fix it yourself."

Now he was fully awake. He feasted with his eyes on her classic form, soft breasts, totally casual in her nakedness, sitting in the rumpled bed beside him. He saw that she had thrown back the sheets off him as well.

He lifted up and kissed one breast. "Good morning," he said.

"Good morning." For a moment she blinked, but one tear slid over a lid and stole down her perfect porcelain cheek.

"I want to thank you, Mr. Morgan, sir. Not since . . ." She caught her breath and blinked again and the words wouldn't come. She shook her head and brushed her eyes, cleared her throat.

"Not for many years have I been with a man the way we were last night. I am truly grateful. Some day I'll explain. If you say anything about this to anyone, I'll shoot you dead."

A moment of anger clouded her eyes, then dissolved. "Oh, dear! I know you would never do that. You must realize that this was a most special and . . . almost sacred experience for me." She sighed, then gracefully lifted up on her knees, bent, and kissed his cheek again.

As natural as a young fawn, she lifted from the bed and dressed. When she was done, he nodded.

"Your dressing was like a ballet, total grace and movement. Planned elegance and form."

"Good," she said, and sat on the bed beside him. "Now I get to watch you dress."

It was no ballet.

She looked at a small gold watch on a gold chain around her neck. "It's nearly ten o'clock. I'll go see the sheriff now. Let's hope that the wanted poster isn't there either. If it isn't, you will only be a lingering memory, until Latimore Potts comes back to town."

She kissed his lips delicately, almost making contact but not firmly. Then she smiled and walked to the door.

"Marybelle's is the best spot in town for breakfast," she said. Then she hurried out, and was down the stairs before he got his gun belt on and his black jacket. He tied the string tie on his way down the stairs, and heard heavy snores coming from two of the small rooms along the hallway. He counted twelve doorknobs.

Downstairs Wally was already behind the bar getting ready for the new day. He said good morning without a trace of any secondary meaning, and Morgan stepped into the sunlight, rubbed his face, and realized he hadn't shaved. It would have to wait. He was starved.

He ate at the cafe quickly, then walked down the familiar street. He was remembering four years ago and a special girl he had known here. He wondered if she was still in town. She had been twenty-one at the time, the new schoolmarm, and they had enjoyed each other's company for two weeks before he'd had to leave quickly. They had kissed only twice and had made no promises. Just the same . . .

He checked the Smith-Jones General Store where the post office used to be. They would know if she was still in town. Milicent Nelson. He would never forget that name. The woman behind the small post office counter was sharp with him. She had seen his tied-down gun and evidently figured he was a gunman.

"Nobody by that name in town," she said quickly when he asked.

"Ma'am, are you sure? She used to be the schoolmistress here back about four years ago. . . ."

The woman nodded. "Milicent, yes, her name did used to be Nelson. I had a son in her classes. She's not a teacher anymore. I can give you her address if you promise she won't come to any harm."

"I'm her friend, nothing more."

The older woman with the gray bun of hair at the back of her head nodded. "She lives at 128 Fourth Street. That's three blocks down and about two north."

He thanked her, and nearly skipped going out the door. Milicent! He had hardly thought of her in four years. He wondered what she was doing now. She had changed her name, which probably meant she was married. So, those things happened.

He walked quickly down the street mindful that he was to be at the saloon at noon. Morgan found the house with no trouble. It was the largest one on the block. He heard a baby cry as he walked up the front porch steps. It was a big house, porch all the way around the front and side, three stories high. He lifted the brass knocker and let it fall.

Somewhere inside he heard movement, then the door opened and a woman stood there, a baby in her arms.

"Yes?"

"Milicent?"

She frowned slightly. "Yes, I'm Milicent Potts. What can I do for you?"

"Milicent . . . Potts? Are you married to the man who used to be sheriff of Cochise County?"

"Yes, that's right, but that was over three years ago."

Morgan took off his hat. "Milicent, I guess you don't remember me."

She gasped, her free hand went to her mouth. "Oh, Dear lord, it's Buckskin Lee Morgan!"

Morgan had his hat in his hands, and he turned it around and around like a lovesick tenderfoot.

"I didn't know you got married."

"Didn't the change in my name give you a hint?"

"The postmistress didn't tell me your last name."

Milicent laughed. "I bet she didn't." She looked at Morgan and sighed. "I didn't say anything about waiting for you."

"I know, I never asked you to. Still, Potts?"

"He's a kind and considerate man."

"And old enough to be your father."

"Not quite, but he's my husband."

"I can plainly see that. Well, Mrs. Potts, I certainly won't bother you anymore." He started to turn, then looked back. "I would appreciate your not saying anything about my being back in town. You know about that wanted poster."

"I do. I had a big fight with him about that. Still, he sent it out."

"I'm here to get that settled once and for all. There was no reason for that wanted."

"I know. Everyone knew. But Latimore was so angry at you. . . ."

"I best be going."

"Yes, that's right, you best."

"Good-bye, Milicent."

He walked away, shaking his head in surprise and anger. Anybody but Potts. She could have married almost anybody but the man who had caused him so much pain.

Morgan was halfway down the block, heading for Allen Street, when the rifle sounded and the slug tore through the top of his hat, sailing it off his head. Morgan dove for the ground and rolled toward the side of a building. Two more rifle shots came, hurried, not aimed well enough.

Morgan tumbled behind the corner of the building, and drew his six-gun and peered around the boards. At first he saw nothing. Then the drifting blue haze from the three rifle shots showed from behind a farm wagon parked across Allen Street. The sniper was far out of six-gun range. But whoever had shot had to show himself to get away from the wagon. There was a blank wall behind the wagon and no other rigs parked along this section of Tombstone's main street.

A buggy came down Fourth Street toward Allen Street, and Morgan saw his chance. In 50 more feet the wagon would be directly between him and the shooter. He crouched there waiting, and when the buggy hit that spot, he raced out and stayed behind it as it rolled along toward Allen Street and the gunman.

The man couldn't shoot through the horse and the buggy. By the time the buggy got to Allen Street Morgan would be well within range of his six-gun. He watched, but saw no movement from anyone leaving the farm wagon.

Another 30 yards and the rig turned sharply to the right, leaving Morgan 40 feet from the farm wagon. Morgan raced toward it, zigzagging, and firing three times at the wagon where traces of the blue smoke still hung in the nearly windless morning.

There was no return fire. Morgan burst around the back of the wagon and stared at the man slumped over the rear wheel. He had an old Sharps rifle with six more rounds on the wagon frame beside him ready to load.

The bushwhacker wasn't moving.

Morgan moved over with his six-gun covering the man. He lifted the man's head from the wagon wheel and saw the blood on the side of it. A small round purpling hole showed in the man's forehead. The .45 slug must have gone in the front and come out the side. The bushwhacker was dead.

Morgan looked around. Two men with guns

drawn walked slowly toward him. He lowered his own revolver and frowned. Now he could see the men clearer and they both wore silver stars.

"Stand easy, stranger, and drop that six-gun. I'm the law in this town and I don't like to see our citizens shot down on the street in broad daylight."

Chapter Five

"This guy fired three rifle shots at me," Morgan said, pushing his six-gun back in his holster. "Didn't you hear a rifle fire?"

The lawman came up, put away his weapon, and checked the dead man. "Huh, Zed Barstow. What's he doing trying to bushwhack someone?"

"You know this man?" Morgan asked.

"Know him, don't know you."

"Name's Morgan. I'm the new guard at the Silver Queen."

"Yeah, I heard. You put down the Sutherland brothers last night. They're mad as hell."

"Mad enough to hire this jasper to kill me?"

"Lots madder than that. This time you're lucky. I saw the whole thing. Me and my officer were coming to question Zed about him shooting here on Allen Street when we spotted you coming. I'll make out a report."

He motioned to the other lawman. "Harry, get this body over to Ritter at the undertakers. I'll keep the rifle as evidence."

The lawman looked up. "Oh, I'm Chief of Police John Inman." He held out his hand. Morgan took it.

"This kind of thing happen often in town?" Morgan asked.

"Seems to. Some folks say Tombstone is the wildest, toughest, deadliest town in the whole damn nation. Might be, and then might not. I hear some of them gold-mining camps bury a man every afternoon."

"You need me any more, Chief?"

"Nope."

"I best get to work. Good meeting you. Sorry it was so official. I'll try to keep from getting shot in your town."

Chief Inman grinned. "I like a man with a sense of humor. Especially one who damn near got himself killed. I'd say you should be a corpse right now instead of Zed here. Most folks know that Zed is about the worst shot in town. Hell, he never could hit the ground with three tries."

"Then why would somebody hire him to gun me?"

"Scare you, not kill you. The Sutherlands are going soft."

"Thanks, Chief Inman. I'm going to be around town for a while."

Morgan hurried along to the Silver Queen and got there in time for the noon meal. He sat down at a table in a big brightly decorated dining room with the 12 fancy ladies. They were in various stages of dress, but didn't seem to mind. They were all covered, but one had on a corset that showed and another only a thin wrapper around her big breasts. They talked among themselves and hardly looked at him.

Miss Lily came in after they had started eating and the girls watched her closely. They saw her smiling, and all seemed to relax.

She sat next to Morgan and frowned. "I checked the wanteds and sure enough, that old one on you is still at the sheriff's office. Sooner or later someone is going to remember you and hook up the name. It could be big trouble for you because it says dead or alive."

"That has been a minor problem a few times in the past."

"I heard about the incident on the street. You think it was the Sutherland brothers?"

"Nobody else in town hates me yet except them and Latimore Potts."

"He tells everyone to call him Senator Potts. He's a senator from this district in the Territorial Legislature."

"That's about as prestigious as playing piano in a bordello." He held up his hands. "No, I don't play the piano." They both laughed and the girls looked up.

"Glad you're laughing, Boss," one of them said.

"Yeah, Boss. I'm glad too," Morgan said. He frowned. "When you won this place, how much cash did you come out ahead for the night?"

"None of your business, but most everyone knows. A little over thirty thousand new money."

"In the bank?"

"Not here. I sent most of it to a bank in Denver I trust." Lily frowned. "Oh, yes. Wally said a letter came for you after you left this morning. Some little boy ran in with it." She handed a short white envelope to Morgan. It was addressed to: "Fast Gunman, The Silver Queen."

Morgan tore open the end of the envelope and pulled out a sheet of paper. He unfolded it and read.

"You don't know me, but I'm in trouble. My husband worked at the Silver Nugget Mine three miles out of town. He worked there for two years, then last week, he didn't come home. Nobody knows where he is. I talked to the mine owner, Mr. Kindermann, and he says he didn't come to work on Friday.

"I know Bret went to work that day. He always does. He's a fine husband. He'd never do anything dishonest. I've heard of other men vanishing at that mine in the past six to eight months. Something is rotten out there.

"Please come and help me. I'll be at Marybelle's Cafe at noon today, I must talk to you."

It was signed "Delsey Tambert."

Morgan let Lily read the letter.

"I've heard of Mrs. Tambert and that her husband is missing. Yes, it's happened at least twice before that I know of. People get killed in the mines all the time. It's a dangerous place to work. But men don't just vanish. The owner out there is Arthur J. Kindermann. I've heard that he's not a nice man."

Morgan held up his hands. "So what should I do?"

Lily laughed. "You already know what you're going to do. A lady in distress. You know nothing gets out of hand in a saloon just after it opens, so you're going to go meet her and see how you can help."

"You wouldn't mind?"

"Morgan, I'd be disappointed in you if you didn't go. As a matter of fact, it's five minutes after twelve already. You better get moving. I've heard that

Delsey is a wonderful lady, and an absolute beauty. So be good."

"I'm always good."

Lily smiled, "I know. Now get out of here."

Five minutes later at Marybelle's Cafe, he found the only lady sitting alone. He asked the man behind the counter if the lady was Delsey Tambert, but he shrugged. Morgan walked over toward her.

She watched him coming. "Mr. Morgan?" she asked.

"Yes, Mrs. Tambert?"

She nodded and motioned for him to sit down. She held out her hand. "I'm Delsey Tambert, Mrs. Taft Tambert. I'm glad you could come. I didn't even know your name when I wrote the note."

"You said your husband is in trouble at the mine?"

Delsey Tambert took a long deep breath and it lifted her bosom. She wore a simple print dress and a light coarse knit sweater. Her long brown hair streamed down her back and she had short bangs across the front. She was maybe 24 or 25. Her face was like one of the Greek statues you see in museums.

"No, Mr. Morgan. I no longer think my husband Taft is in trouble. I'm sure that he's dead. Two other men have worked in the same mine, doing about the same job. They have been missing for over a year now, and nothing has ever been found of either of them. I'm through crying. Now I want to find out exactly how my husband was killed, who did it and why. I . . . I don't have a lot of money, but you can have all I own, almost two hundred dollars. And besides that, I'll . . ." She stopped, took another deep breath and hurried on, her voice low, but forced. "And I'll be your mistress as long as you want."

Morgan lifted his brows. "Mrs. Tambert, there's no reason to talk about any kind of payment. I have a job, I have some money of my own. I might look into these disappearances as a public service. First tell me where the mine is and what work your husband did."

She nodded, face serious, her beautiful features working into a frown.

"Taft worked at the Silver Nugget Mine, three miles out of town in the hills of the San Pedro River. He started in the tunnels, then when they found out he was good doing his numbers, they moved him to a better job, and six months ago he went to work in the place where they get the silver out of the mashed-up ore and it's poured into bars. I've never understood it all that well.

"That's about it. Last Thursday he went to work, but he didn't come home the way he usually does about seven in the evening. I sat up all night. The next morning I got a horse and rode out to the mine, but the owner made me wait two hours to talk to him, then he said he didn't know anything about where Taft was. Said no one was reported hurt or injured the previous day. He took me to the man who Taft had worked for. He swore that Taft did his shift and left the building about six-thirty the day before.

"I think they both were lying. The foreman, he didn't do a good job of it at all. But what could I do?"

"Did you talk to the sheriff?"

"No, he was out of town, but I talked to one of his deputies and we filled out a missing-man report and he said he certainly would do all that he could. Which has been exactly nothing. So when I heard you were in town and that you bootstrapped those two mean Sutherland brothers, I figured you were the man to find out what happened to Taft. I know he's dead, I just want to know for sure what happened, and to punish anyone who was responsible."

Morgan had a hard time concentrating on what the lady said. She was a striking, classic beauty, and even now in sorrow and anger, she was magnificent. He looked away from her face and listened to the words. She had stopped now and he nodded.

"Mrs. Tambert, I'll see what I can do. I'm working on another matter as well and I'm not sure how much time I have. . . ."

She put her hand on his arm and he felt sparks fly. Her warm touch persisted. "Mr. Morgan. I am an honest woman. I said you may come to my house now or anytime and I will lay with you. It's a simple matter of fairness. In all honesty I can't guarantee you my passion, but certainly my cooperation. Do you understand?"

Morgan smiled at her and covered her hand with his. "Mrs. Tambert, I understand. There is no need for any payment. The offer is tremendously tempting because you are the most strikingly beautiful lady I have seen in a long, long time. You have a classic beauty that most men would kill for. For now all we need is a handshake, and I'll do what I can. I hate to see rich, powerful men ride rough and mean over those they control."

"Thank you!" She smiled, and Morgan almost fell at her feet in worship. "I do have to get back now. I have washing to do."

"Washing?" he asked. "I don't understand."

"Mr. Morgan, we must be realistic. I'm a widow with no means of support. So I put up a sign and now I take in washing. I must make a living."

"Yes, of course."

She stood up and so did he.

"Let me walk you home. Then I'll know where to contact you."

Tombstone had grown dramatically since it began in February of 1879. Now with the mines booming there were more than 7,000 people in the community. The main street, Allen, was more than four blocks long, and houses had sprouted and grown like mushrooms on both sides.

The Tambert home was small, painted white, and three blocks from Allen.

"We . . . I'm renting the house. I'll probably take in one or two single women as borders. That way, and by doing washing, I should be able to survive."

"There's more to life than surviving, Mrs. Tambert. I'm going to see that you have a just settlement from this Mr. Kindermann." She smiled faintly and he said good-bye.

Business was slow back at the Silver Queen Saloon. Morgan took his favorite rear table and sipped at a cool beer. A few minutes later Lily came out and sat in the chair beside him.

"Morgan, about last night."

"Last night was a tender, and beautiful moment that I'm going to remember for a long, long time. I was touched, I was moved, I felt totally in tune and harmony with another human being."

Lily looked up at him with tears in her eyes. She wiped them away and wiped her nose then stared at him. "Oh, God, what woman was it, Morgan, who let you get away? How could she have been so stupid? She should have caught you around the ankle and not let go, making you drag her every step you took. Women are so damn idiotic!"

They sat there a moment watching each other, and then they both chuckled. Lily shook her head. "Morgan, I don't know about you. Right now you have the wrong slant on me. From last night you think one thing, but now I need to show you just how low and dirty and sexy and whorish I can get. That would balance things out."

He reached over and put his fingers across her lips. "Hush. I knew a wise lady once in Abilene. She told me the first rule is never tell anyone, especially a spouse, anything you don't have to. She was a madam, had a record of marrying off more than half of her girls and sending them home with trail-drive cowboys and ranch owners.

"She told her girls and their husbands never to tell a damn thing about the lady's background. Whore no more was the key. I guess what I'm saying is, what they don't know won't hurt them. If you ever get out of here and latch onto some big-city millionaire, don't you dare tell him or anyone else that you owned the Silver Queen. Remember, damnit! That's rule number one!"

Her brows shot up and mouth opened in a soft "Oh," and then she nodded. "Yes, I can agree with that. Now, what about the striking Mrs. Tambert? Are you going to help her? First let me tell you that Kindermann is the dog that wags the tail around here. He has the biggest, richest silver mine in the county.

"He owns about half the firms in town and has half a dozen investors who own shares in the Silver Nugget Mine. Some say he also owns the sheriff, but nobody has ever proved that. What I'm saying is Kindermann is a tough man to pick a fight with."

"Thanks for the background. He's just the kind of bastard I like to chop down to size and smash in the face with my fists. The lady said three men have now vanished at that same mine with no trace ever found of them. Have you heard that?"

"Sure. But mining is a damned dangerous way to

earn a living."

"But these men worked above ground—in the refining operation, I'd guess."

"Oh, then that would be unusual."

"To answer your question, I think I will nose around a little and see what I can dig up. Who is the best-informed person in town? Somebody who isn't cowed by the big mine owners, and who can think on his feet?"

Lily grinned. "I have just the man for you. Brawley Goodrich, the editor of the Tombstone *Nugget*, the other newspaper in town. He fits your description to the letter."

Morgan stood. "Things won't get mean around here until after six tonight. Think I'll go see Mr. Goodrich for a small talk."

Lily nodded. "Thought you would, or I never would have mentioned his name. Be careful of those runty little Sutherland brothers."

Chapter Six

The Tombstone *Nugget*, the smaller of the town's two newspapers, was housed in a niche between a men's clothing store and a saddlemaker's shop of fine-smelling leathers. Morgan sniffed on the way past, then turned into the newspaper office and found a man sitting behind a desk. His feet rested on the corner of the desk, his fingers were laced together behind his head, and he stared out the window.

"Good afternoon, if I'm not disturbing you," Morgan said.

"Hell, yes, you're disturbing me, but you already have, so go ahead."

"Thanks. Looking for a polecat named Brawley Goodrich."

The man opened his eyes but didn't move otherwise. He stared at Morgan for a minute, then nodded. "You found him. Sit a spell and rest your shanks mare. I been doing some contemplating, mostly about you. Thoughtful of you to walk right in this way."

Morgan sat in the offered chair. The editor was a wiry guy, probably no more than five-six with carrot-red hair, the worst red mustache Morgan had ever seen, and the rest of the crop of red whiskers close shaven.

"Some say this Lee Morgan is a famous gun-sharp. Others say he came to town on a white stallion ready to rescue a fair maiden. Me, I figure to wait and watch a while. Oh, nice bit of shooting this morning nailing old Zed. Not a great loss to the town. Zed was one of our town drunks. Couldn't hit his hat with his head. You know who sicked him on you?"

"The Brothers Sutherland is my best bet."

"You'd win." Brawley took his feet off the desk, slid back in the chair, and stared at Morgan. "Why are you in town, Mr. Morgan?"

"Business. This a good town to start a business in?"

"Good for a gun-for-hire business. Wouldn't wonder but what you can use that Colt, tied as low as it is. You a gunfighter?"

"Not when I can help it. About like any other man."

"Not entirely true, Morgan. I've seen the way you move down a street. Not a walk exactly, more like a stalking. You always know who is around you, your eyes take in the whole street, and I bet you could spot a rifle muzzle at fifty yards if it was pointed at you."

"I didn't this morning. He got off the first shots."

"But you nailed him with the last ones."

"I understand you're an honest man, Brawley. Folks tell me you call a man by his true colors even if he don't like the shade of your paint brush. What's the score on Kindermann."

"Ha! You are after bigger game than a Zed Barstow. I knew it. You just might be a help to the town after all. Brother Kindermann has money, borrowed money from six investors to help him get the Silver Nugget in operation. You know the old saying. You have to own a gold mine to operate a silver mine. Damn expensive, but it pays off in the long run with silver ingots."

"Heard he owns half the town."

"About right. He don't own me."

"Good. You hear about Taft Tambert?"

"Did. That makes three."

"What's going on out there?"

"Murder most foul, as our English friends would say. A bushwhacking of the first water."

"Who and why?" Morgan asked.

"Ah, ha, two of the five questions of the good journalist. Who, what, when, where, and why. We know who got killed, about when, and near enough where. But who did it and why was he dropped down a dry shaft? Just my theory, of course, Mr. Morgan."

"Good theory. Does Kindermann mine, crush, and smelter out the silver right on his property up there?"

"Sure does. One of the latest processes. He uses the cyanide process up there. Not too complex. He showed me how it works one day. Saves shipping all that silver ore anywhere else to get it processed."

"Which means that Kindermann winds up with more profit."

"Damn true. Nothing illegal about that."

"The American way, like making money on a

newspaper. How is it going here against your competition?"

"I'm still operating. Want to buy in for, say, twenty thousand dollars?"

"No."

They both laughed.

"How are the Sutherland brothers tied in with Kindermann?"

"Nobody has proved that they are. But you're probably right. I've been trying to get enough real evidence and factual material on that question for six months."

"So far all I've heard is that Kindermann is a good mining owner, a good businessman, and knows how to manage his people," Morgan said.

"He's also ruthless, takes what and who he wants, and usually lets little time pass before he goes after anything that he wants to take over."

"A question. The other two men who died in the mine, or around it, and vanished. Did they by any chance have young, attractive wives?"

"Not as beautiful as Delsey Tambert. But yes, they were young and attractive, and as far as I know, both of them wound up in Kindermann's bedroom for various lengths of time."

"Then what happened to them?"

"No one seems to know."

"They vanished too?"

"Seems to be the case."

"Neither of the other two had any children?"

"No, same as Delsey."

"Damn, this is taking on a decidedly deadly turn. You know anyone who works in the Silver Nugget who's honest and would talk?"

"I've been looking for six months, and I can't find anyone who isn't so frightened that he won't even admit he works at the Silver Nugget."

"That cuts down on the possibilities, doesn't it?"

"Which means you can't go in yourself, Morgan. Your two little acts of bravado have identified you to half the town, and certainly Kindermann has heard of you by now. He has his ear to the goings-on here in Tombstone. In fact, he has a big house at the edge of town."

"He does? And he's gone all day?"

"I wouldn't try it, not even if I had nine lives to work with."

"Brawley, you're the kind of guy who wants to live forever."

"Great idea. If you find out anything, I get the story first, agreed?"

Morgan left the newspaper office by the back door, hurried from one building to another, and watched behind him as much as he looked ahead. By the time he was within a block of Mrs. Tambert's house he decided no one had followed him.

He knocked on the just-painted front door and saw Delsey coming forward. Through a curtained glass window in the door he could see her touching her hair.

She opened the panel and waved him inside as a smile blossomed on her pretty face.

"So soon? Have you learned something so quickly?"

"I have. Do you still have that two hundred dollars?"

"Yes, do you want it?"

"Oh, no. You're going to need it. Let's sit down, we need to talk."

She took him into the front room with its inexpensive furniture that was bright and clean. Delsey was as delicious as he remembered, a true beauty. With a little bit of stage makeup she would be stunning. He marveled at the easy motion of her hips under the tight print dress. They sat on a sofa.

"You said two other men vanished up at the Silver Nugget, remember?"

"Yes, I knew one of them."

"Did you know his wife?"

"Yes, Patricia, an attractive girl, tall and slender, but with a fine woman's figure."

"Whatever happened to Patricia?"

"Come to think of it, I don't know. She told me one day that she was going to Phoenix, and I never saw her again."

"No one else has either. I have learned that Arthur J. Kindermann took Patricia and the other widow of the man lost in his mine to his bed. Both of them served him in his bedroom until he grew tired of them."

Delsey jumped back, her face a frown of anger and surprise. "You can't be serious. Are you suggesting that he killed their husbands just so he could . . . It's too horrible to even consider."

"Delsey, I suggest you consider it strongly. There have been rumors, and stories, but not enough actual evidence for anyone to put together a case against Kindermann."

"In this modern day such an act by an important man is simply unthinkable," Delsey protested. She scowled. "He couldn't get away with it. Someone would know."

"More than one man knows, I'm sure, but they are afraid to talk. Life in a deep rock mine is cheap, easily lost." He reached out and caught both of her shoulders with his hands. "Delsey, what I'm saying is that you yourself are in danger. At any time now, you could be tricked into going up to the mine, probably at night, probably in a closed carriage. You might also be told to advise your closest friend that you were going to Phoenix."

Her eyes filled with tears. She shook her head. "I can't believe it! I simply can't believe it could be true."

"Do you have any friends in Phoenix?"

"Yes, but . . ."

"Delsey, I suggest that tomorrow morning you and I take the stage heading for Phoenix. As I remember, it leaves about six in the morning. You'll have to be up early."

"I . . . I don't know."

"Where are your savings, in the bank?"

"Oh, no, I don't trust the bank. It's here, in gold."

"Good, pack a small bag, don't try to take too much. Wear something that comes up high around your neck and a big hat that will cover your face. Use a veil if you want to. We don't want anyone to know that you're leaving."

"But my life has been here. We were married here . . . I only have one aunt in Phoenix."

"Better to start over there than to wind up at the bottom of one of the four-hundred-foot shafts in the Silver Nugget Mine. That's probably where the other two wives are right now."

Delsey shuddered. She leaned against him and her arms went around him. "Why are you doing this for me?"

"You need help, you asked me. Besides, I have a sense of rage against men like Kindermann. I enjoy stopping them from doing any more of their bloody deeds."

She settled against him, her breasts pressing into his shirt. Her arms held him tightly. She spoke with her face against his chest and he could barely hear her.

"Mr. Morgan. I'll go under two conditions. You must not go all the way to Phoenix. We'll make Tucson in one long day. You must leave the coach there." She looked up at him. "And second, you must stay here tonight and let me show you my total physical appreciation for what you are doing. You must let me make love to you."

She reached up and kissed his lips. It was soft, gentle, like a breath of spring flowers. He drank in the scent of her, and when her lips left his again he returned the kiss and the thrill of a perfect love swept through him.

He pushed her away gently. "First you must pack. Keep everything as usual. I'll go out the front door in case anyone is watching your place. As soon as it's dark, I'll be back here."

She watched him, disbelief crowding onto her beautiful face. "I can't figure out why you're doing all this for me. We were strangers until this morning."

"Delsey, it just has to be. Now remember, act naturally the rest of the day. I'll be back as soon as it gets dark. Bar the front and back doors and lock all the windows. If anyone comes to the door, tell them you have the German measles and you can't come out. Promise?"

She nodded. Delsey reached up and kissed him once more. "I'll never be able to repay you, Mr. Morgan. I truly never will."

"You get away to Phoenix and it will be pay enough to see the anger and frustration on Kindermann's face when he finds out he's missed you." He turned and walked to the front door. On the porch, he turned and looked back in the house and talked in a loud voice.

"Well, then, Mrs. Tambert, I'll have to look for lodging elsewhere. I didn't know you were asking for female boarders only. Good day to you."

Morgan turned and walked away. He watched every bush and the grounds around each house he passed, but he could see no one watching her place. If Kindermann would just wait another day or two, Morgan would have Delsey out of here and safely away. Another of the damned ifs.

Morgan strode quickly toward the saloon. He watched the doors now and the alleys, his right hand always near his gun. A few men stared at him, and when he stared back at them, they glanced away.

He went up the alley and into the back door of the Silver Queen. Everything was quiet in the saloon. He found Miss Lily and told her what he had learned and about his sudden desire to see Tucson.

"Kindermann is a real bastard!" Lily said scowling. "I'd heard that the two women had left town. I didn't realize that he had been involved with the widows. He must have had to kill them after that."

"I'm sure he did. Either him or one of his men. He must be rich. Why does he need to do all this?"

"Some men go crazy in strange ways. He has to be insane to kill three men just to get their wives in his bed. The man deserves to be castrated and then roasted head down over a fire the way the Comanches used to do."

"Even that sounds too good for him," Morgan said. "My big problem now is how to prove it well enough for my own satisfaction."

"You're not talking about courtroom evidence?"

"I've never been one to hold with a strict interpretation of the law. I like the Biblical eye-for-an-eye kind of justice. A one-man kind of justice, jury, judge, and executioner all rolled into one."

"If what you suspect is true, half the people in town would like to help drop the trap on that bastard."

They talked the rest of the afternoon. At last he eased the conversation back to Lily. "You said your

pa was still alive but you didn't talk much to him.
The poet and all. You having any second thoughts
about home?"

"Sure, a few. I'm three years older now. Hell, a
woman learns a lot in three years, especially on the
fast road to hell I've been charging down.

"Just never can tell how a parent is going to react.
My daddy could be changeable as all hell."

They sipped at their beers.

"Wonder if I could find that poet guy," Morgan
said. "I mean, just as a for-wondering question.
Wonder what happened to him. Suppose he's still
around your old hometown? Maybe he ran off with
some preacher's wife or something by now since
you didn't stay."

Miss Lily laughed. "Hartley just might do something like that. Though I think he'd pick some
woman with lots of money."

"You didn't have any money."

She hesitated, then shrugged. "No, but my daddy
did. My daddy was a big man in the town where we
lived, and it was a pretty big town. I wonder if good
old Hartley loved me for my daddy's money?"

"Stranger things have happened, Miss Lily. Much,
much stranger."

Chapter Seven

A half hour after full dark, Morgan lay beside a vacant house four doors down and across the street from the Tambert home. He had been there for ten minutes, and waited another half hour watching the Tambert place. So far there had been no sign that the house was being observed by anyone.

He invested another ten minutes, then filtered across the street and between houses to come up behind Delsey's house. He put in another half hour watching the back of the house and the surrounding area.

Nothing moved.

Morgan slipped like a dark cloud from one cover to another, then up to the back door. It was unlocked and no light was on in the room beyond it.

He slipped inside and waited a moment, then locked the door and put a chair under the handle. There was no bar for the door.

He called softly from the darkened room. It was the kitchen, he decided. Morgan went to the closed door toward the front and called softly again.

"Delsey, it's Morgan."

There was a gasp, then rushing feet and the woman was in his arms. Sobs shook her slender body. He held her close and realized she wore only a nightgown.

"I've been so frightened!" she sobbed. "I kept hearing all sorts of noises. Then I'd think again about Kindermann and the other two wives. So horrible!"

"Is the front door locked?"

"Yes, and it has a bar across it. I locked all of the windows, but I thought how easily they could be broken. And I kept the back door unlocked for you."

"Don't worry about anything now. Were you getting dressed?"

"No, I was getting ready for you."

"You're sure about this?"

"Oh, yes! I'm a grown woman, an adult, and I need to pay my debts. I made an agreement. I have to stand by it."

He felt her move against him, her hips hard against his, her flat tummy pushing against him, her breasts so tight on his chest that he could feel her heartbeat.

His voice came out husky. "Delsey, where is your bedroom?"

He felt her body react, a small shiver, then she pressed harder at him. Hot blood surged in his veins. He could feel a swelling at his crotch.

She reached up in the darkness and found his lips and kissed him. It was a simple song of love that he tasted, an echoing of passion and tenderness and caring that had come down through the ages of man. Gently he picked her up, one arm under her bent knees and the other around her shoulders. She clung to him, and directed him through another door, where he found a blanket over the window and four candles burning in the bedroom.

He let her down to stand on the floor and she looked up at him shyly. "I thought candlelight would be delightful."

"Yes, it's good." He touched her shoulder and she shivered.

"Lee, Lee Morgan, would you . . . could you pretend to . . . love me just for tonight?"

Morgan smiled. Every woman he had bedded he had loved a little, even if for just a few hours. The mere physical act was never enough for him. There had to be more and a deep sense of love had to come, even if quickly.

He bent and kissed her softly on her lips. "Delsey, I do love you, for your honest nature, for your loyalty and outrage at Kindermann, for your exquisite beauty of mind and body."

"Oh, my!" She pulled him toward the bed and sat there, and kissed him so hard it almost pushed him over. He felt her breasts against him now, and soon her hands unbuttoned his shirt and slid inside, and she sighed but never let the kiss go. Her mouth opened and his responded. Her tongue was a flame darting in and out.

Delsey sighed and opened her eyes and let the kiss end, and pushed her arms under his shirt around him and hugged him tightly.

"Yes, yes!"

She came away from him, and he pushed one hand to her chest and covered one breast. She watched him and nodded.

"That feels good, Lee, feels so wonderful."

He caressed them, then reached down the full neckline. His hand closed over one of her bare bosoms, and she shivered again and gasped and leaned against him. Then slowly she bent and eased backward to the bed.

"Sweet Lee. I love your hands on me. It's so right." She reached up and unbuttoned his shirt, and he sat up and took it and the light jacket off and leaned over her. She pulled him down and nibbled at his man breasts, and as she did, Delsey unbuttoned his fly.

She pushed him away, sat up, and then stood in front of him and slowly lifted the soft white nightgown off over her head. He marveled at the sculptured, perfect legs. So purely white, so soft and unmarked with smooth, sleek inner thighs right up to the swatch of dark hair.

Then he saw the small mound and then a flat, tight little stomach swelling with her rib cage to delightfully large breasts. Her nipples were swollen already, a deep red against pale pink areolas.

Over her strong chest was her slender, elegant neck, and then the perfect face with its classic, finely chiseled beauty.

No words were spoken. She knelt and finished unbuttoning his fly, then pulled down his pants and his short underwear. He was hard by then, fully erect and throbbing. She smiled at his manhood, reached out and caressed it, stroked him a few times, then sat him down on the bed and pulled off his boots and the rest of his clothes.

"Stand beside me," she said.

He stood and she pressed her naked flesh against his, from knees and thighs, hips and crotch and bellies up to her breasts against his chest. Her head rested against his shoulder and he held her tightly.

"Morgan, you don't have to seduce me. I'm ready now if you want me."

He eased away from her and kissed her eyes, then her nose, and then deeply her mouth. When the boiling kiss was through he smiled at her in the candlelight.

"I want to seduce you, to bring you to the fiery need of it. That will be more satisfying for you, and perhaps give you a better memory of this terrible week."

He picked her up and lay her gently on the bed. Then he lay half over her and caressed her and kissed her lips, her open mouth, and then her throat. She moaned softly as he trailed a line of hot kisses down her chest to her breast. He attacked her swollen nipples at once, kissing them and sucking on them, then nibbling and at last biting them until she yelped once in surprise.

"Oh, Lord, but you are fine! That is so . . . so . . . good!"

He worked over her other breast. Then his hand wandered down her torso and stopped at her small mound just above her crotch.

"Morgan that feels wonderful. You have talented hands. Oh, God! Touch me there again." She wailed low and soft, a throaty sound that spoke of raw passion.

Her hand found his crotch and caught hold of his maleness and held on.

Gently he passed the mound and trailed one hand lightly over her crotch. She gasped when his fingers brushed her soft, moist nether lips.

"Oh . . . God . . . yes!" Her hips humped at him three times. "Christ! Oh . . . fuck!"

His fingers found her and brushed the swollen red

lips again, parted them, and pushed in an inch or so. Her hips rose to meet him and she keened lightly a high, surging sound that gave vent to a million feelings of the primal ancestors who had coupled out of instinct and not need before the two had become tangled and intertwined until now no one could tell the difference.

"Please, darling Lee, come in me now!"

He waited, trailing his hand down her soft velvet thigh, then back up the other one. He surged over her heartland and found the small hard node and brushed it, then hit it harder and twanged it side to side six times.

"Oh . . . oh . . . oh . . . ohhhhhhhhhhhhhhhhhh. I'm going to! I can't stop!" She shrilled into a strange wild cry, and then her whole body shook with spasms that darted through her, jolting and jerking and stiffening her body as the climax rolled through her again and again until he lost count. He kept twanging her clit until she put down one hand and pushed him away.

Only then did she taper off and open her eyes and stare up at him, sweat on her forehead, hair tangled around her face, and a look of absolute wonder.

"How in the world . . ." She shook her head. "It doesn't matter."

She pushed him away, lifted to a sitting position beside him, and bent to his crotch. She kissed the purpled head of his manhood, then licked it until it jerked from the caress. Slowly, gradually she let the arrowhead of him slip between her lips until she had him firmly mouthed. She moved up and down on him, taking in more and more until her lips touched his brown crotch fur. Still she bobbed and he stared in amazement.

His hips began to lift and pound, and quickly he

was at a point where he knew he couldn't stop.

"Do you want to take it there?" he asked between pantings.

"Uh-huh" she said around his maleness, as she bobbed up and down.

He could stand it no longer. Gently as he could, he humped upward at her, felt the rockets go off, felt the primal instincts fulfilled as his seed shot out into her envelope, her unusual depository.

The stars exploded, and he panted and roared and then bellowed his domination over this mere female, and he gushed his last planting and then lifted her off him and lay her on the pillows of the bed, and bent and kissed her lips as he fell beside her, spent and drained and comatose.

Delsey snuggled against him, one hand across his chest, her head on his shoulder, one hand holding his wilting manhood. Neither of them spoke for ten minutes. Then she roused and moved over him. She spread his legs and lay between them, lowering one big breast into his mouth. He took it automatically.

It was ripe and warm and he sucked on it and chewed delicately, until she moaned and crooned a small song. Down below, her hand worked at his limp tool. Slowly he came to life, and then he surged into excited attention.

"Get me ready," she whispered in his ear, and took one of his hands to her dark muff. He explored, found her slot, and caressed it, rubbed it on the outside and then probed deep into her, bringing out her juices, lathering them on her swollen, red nether lips until she squirmed.

"Yes, yes. You know just what to do." She moved his hand and held his lance just right, and then with a shriek of intense pleasure lowered onto him, driving his erection deep into her vagina.

"Oh, Lord! Oh! Oh! Damn, but that is deep! Christ! So good, darling Morgan, so good!"

She leaned on her hands near his shoulders, and her knees were brought up near his hips. She bent forward and her hips came with her and she rocked back and forth, and then soon she was riding him like a wild stallion on the open range.

She panted and her hair fell around her face. She blew it away and bucked and rode him, panting faster now, sweat beading on her forehead, her breasts swinging past him with each long stroke as she milked him and pounded, doing all of the work, letting him rest.

The second time had always been slowest for Morgan. He had to work at it. Now he helped. He bucked upward each time she came down and he pushed forward when she levered back. Soon they had worked out a mutually beneficial system, and Delsey groaned and grunted now with each stroke.

She watched him, and her tongue came out as she panted. Saliva dripped off her tongue onto his chest. He reached up and grabbed a soft handful of each of his buttocks and slammed her down each time he came up.

They matched a new stroke, new timing.

"Come on, make it, you fucker!" she growled at him. "I'm giving you all I've got to give." Suddenly she started crying. Tears gushed from her eyes and dripped on him as she kept pounding.

"I love you, you big cock! I love you and want you to come stay with me in Phoenix. Together we can do anything. You're so beautiful, so handsome, so manly. I want you forever!"

Somehow her voice tripped his switch and he grunted and bellowed in release, and a few strokes later he was done and she fell on him in delight and exhaustion, panting as fast and hard as he was.

Morgan wanted to say something but he couldn't. He closed his eyes.

It was an hour before either of them awoke. The candles had burned down to the cups they sat in and were almost out. He roused and she rolled off him, watching him closely.

He bent and kissed her lips, then both her eyes. "Wonderful," he said.

She nodded her dark eyes judging him in the semi-darkness. "Yes, wonderful." She lay there a moment looking up at him where he hovered over her.

"Are you hungry? I have some fresh bread and some cheese and some homemade jelly."

Five minutes later they sat on the floor in the bedroom. She had brought a napkin and spread out the food, and they ate and touched each other and ate again. Morgan couldn't stop from touching her. At the moment he wanted nothing else but to hold her, to touch her, to watch her, to marvel at her exquisite body and her astounding, beautiful face. She was a woman almost any man would kill to possess. He understood Kindermann's desire. He also despised the man.

"You'll get off the stage in Tucson?"

"Yes, if you feel safe there."

She reached under the mattress and pulled out a side-by-side derringer.

"It's a .45-caliber and I have extra rounds," Delsey said. "I'll feel plenty safe by that time."

"Have you ever shot it?"

"Oh, yes. I fired twenty rounds through it the day I bought it. With Taft gone so long each day, I figured I needed something more than that flimsy lock on the door."

"Take that with you. Why don't you pack one bag now to take along tomorrow. As you do, I'll have a short nap."

"Hey, that last time I did all the work."

Morgan grinned. "And you were wonderful at it. Do you have any more of that good cheese?"

Chapter Eight

Arthur J. Kindermann threw a pad of paper across the room and glared at the man who had just walked into his office with a report.

"What the hell do you mean, there's nobody home?" Kindermann thundered. "Where could she be? Of course there has to be somebody home."

Kindermann was a big man, an inch over six feet at a time when five-six was the average height. He had thick blond hair starting to gray and bushy eyebrows. He wore a full beard carefully trimmed, and now his eyes were glaring at the messenger.

The man trembled, but stood up to the angry man the best he could. "I did what you said, but she was gone. One of her neighbors said she saw a light in the kitchen about five this morning, and later it went out and she saw two people leave, one of them, the woman, with a traveling bag.

"I checked the stage office. Two couples left on the stage heading for Phoenix this morning. Can't be sure who either of them were. The clerk was new and said he didn't recognize them as they bought tickets."

"Damn! God damnit! Everything was going so well. All right, get back to your regular job. Aren't you a guard on the night shift?"

The man nodded.

"Just see that you do your job, and anybody fooling around where they aren't supposed to be, like around the reduction plant or those off-limits tunnels, you shoot first and we'll see who it was later."

"Yes, sir, Mr. Kindermann." The guard hurried out, looking relieved to leave the mine owner's office.

Kindermann drew circles and squares on a pad of paper on his desk, then slashed through them with heavy strokes and ripped off the page and threw it on the floor.

He had been looking forward to some diversion this afternoon with the magnificent Delsey Tambert. It wasn't going to happen. Either something scared her off or she was one day ahead of him in deciding to move. She probably had people in Phoenix. What the hell, so did he. He might send a message to Phoenix. He could still make an effort, but hell, maybe it wasn't worth the trouble. In a town like Tombstone, there were plenty of women who would kick up their heels and pull off their clothes.

Two such women worked for him in his outer office. One was his bookkeeper and the other kept track of the men's hours and made out their pay envelopes every week. Martha was the older of the two. She had been a delight for almost a year for him, a wildcat in bed, usually wore him right down to a nub. Then she'd committed the unpardonable sin of getting pregnant.

The other girl, Jenny, was barely eighteen, and still ready to fill in on his social calendar if need be. She wasn't as passionate as Martha, but she had a much better body, a slender waist and sleek legs and big tits. He walked through the offices now, stopped at Jenny's desk, and patted her shoulder. She looked up, and he reached down through the scoop-necked dress she wore and cupped one of her fine bare breasts. He tweaked her nipple and felt it harden.

"I might want you to work late tonight, little darling Jenny," he said softly.

"My pleasure . . . Mr. Kindermann." She looked up at him. "That feels so good, Mr. Kindermann."

"It certainly does. Yes. You stay late tonight." He pulled his hand away, and she adjusted her dress and smiled at him as he walked away.

Martha waited until Kindermann had left the room, then hurried over to Jenny and laughed softly. "I'll be damned. The virgin queen is getting fucked again tonight. That's twice this week. The old boy must be getting hard up."

Jenny only smiled. "Not hard up enough to pick you, Martha. Too bad. It's been so long for you you're probably a virgin again." Then both of them laughed. In spite of their both wanting to go to bed with Kindermann, they were really best friends.

Martha chuckled. "You tell me all about it tomorrow, every fucking little detail."

Jenny grinned. "Don't worry. That's half the fun."

Meanwhile, Kindermann continued out of the mine office, across the hot, dusty Arizona landscape to the reduction plant. He had decided early on to set up a complete mining process there. That meant the mine itself, the stamping mills to smash the ore down into workable-sized solids, and then the chemical plant to get the silver out of the ore.

The process was simple and relatively new. He had been involved in mining silver in Virginia City, and was determined not to make the mistakes the owners made there.

He brought in a plant to use the cyanide process. It could be used only on ore that held only silver or silver and gold. First he pulverized the silver ore, and then leached it with a dilute sodium cyanide water solution. The silver formed a water-soluble sodium-silver complex.

That mixture was then filtered, and the solids that remained were useless and discarded. The filtered mixture was next treated with finely divided zinc dust that caused the silver to precipitate from the solution.

This precipitate was then filtered off, melted, cast into bullion bars, and was ready for sale.

Only his most trusted men worked in the reduction plant. Here was the end product of all the rest of the activity. The work of 500 men could be stolen in ten minutes without proper supervision at this end.

Every time the precipitate was melted down and cast, he was present. As a result he could say with certainty that he had not lost an ounce of silver since his operation there began. He had the records to prove it.

The silver bars were the most gloriously beautiful sight on earth. When they cooled and came out of the molds and were stamped with the date with hammer and die, he felt a thrill that was unlike anything in the world.

Sex was not even in the same category with viewing a stack of silver bars from his own mine.

He nodded to the various workers, went on through the large room filled with vats and the processes, and came to the room where the filtrate was melted down and cast into bars.

His arrival was the signal to begin the process, and he watched and waited as the furnace quickly melted one large iron pot of silver after another. The pouring was the dangerous part. One man had had a foot burned completely off last year when he made a stupid mistake and a mold overflowed molten silver on his foot.

The liquid silver had burned his shoe like it was paper, and then sizzled and charred his flesh down to the bone before they got buckets of water dumped on his foot.

Since then they had taken precautions. That accident would not happen again. He watched, fascinated as the filtrate melted in the big pots. The first pouring into the molds went well, then a second, and a third.

He sat in a big, soft chair he had arranged to have there, and watched the process. Nobody could steal the molten silver, but a man could let drips hit the ground and later, when they were cold, scoop them up. The molds were placed on large steel plates so this could not happen. All spillage was allowed to cool, then picked up and put back in the melting pots.

Three hours later the pouring was finished and the silver had cooled and the forms were being removed. Each of the casting forms had the words

"Silver Nugget" in them so the imprint was left on every ingot.

Besides that, a number and date were stamped into the soft metal with a die and a hammer.

Now even that work was finished, and the men were sent to their other jobs until more silver was ready to melt. Kindermann was alone with his tally man.

The tally man was the most important one in the plant. He recorded the number of ingots cast and the dates of each. The tally man was also Kindermann's worst problem. Each time the ten pound bars of silver were cast, a certain number were not recorded. They were stamped and dated, but they were set to one side.

Then the tally man and Kindermann loaded the unrecorded bars on a pushcart and moved the cart down a connecting tunnel to a large "room" dug out of the ground during normal mining operations. There they unloaded the silver bars and stacked them under canvas covers.

All this was done directly from the recovery building into the mine tunnel, and no one ever saw them do it. It was a silver treasure trove that Kindermann kept only for himself.

Kindermann's six partners never knew of the silver bars that he was skimming off the top of the production. He averaged about 20 percent of the production. That was as much as he figured he could steal without them finding out. However, the tally man knew all about it. Bribes usually worked. If not, loyalty and the threat of losing the man's job often did the trick. Over the four years of operation, there had been several different workers who had been tally men who'd had unfortunate accidents.

The tally man's job was not one that was sought

after. Taft Tambert had been the last tally man to have an accident. He would not take a bribe, not even when he was offered 50 dollars each time the silver bars were stored away. Too bad, really.

Kindermann had tried to think of some way he could do the whole job himself, but nothing seemed to work.

The current tally man, Lenny Nadler, had accepted the bribe eagerly. In fact he had asked for the position, and it looked like he would be around for a while. Unless he got greedy. They poured silver twice a week, and an extra $100 a week was far, far more money than any other worker in the mine made.

Another crew came when the skimming was done and, again under Kindermann's personal supervision, put the silver bars in the big bank vault safe he had installed in another tunnel dug into the mountain directly from the side of the reduction plant building. A thousand pounds of dynamite wouldn't even budge the door on that vault. The rear of the tunnel had been blasted shut so there was no way to get to the vault from the rear.

At infrequent and random intervals Kindermann led heavily loaded wagons on the 70-mile drive to Tucson and then on to Phoenix. Some of these wagons had silver on them and some didn't. He had never lost a load of silver heading for the train at Phoenix and his consignment to the U.S. Treasury.

With the silver safely stored away, Kindermann went back to his office, which was adjoining a three-room apartment he had built for himself there. Many times he slept over, and he would tonight.

He unlocked the main office building and went in, then through the dark rooms to his private suite door, which he unlocked and entered.

Two lamps burned in the small sitting room. More light came from the large bedroom. He walked to the door and looked in. Jenny lay on the bed, naked, eating from a bunch of grapes. She saw him and held the grapes out to him.

Kindermann laughed softly and entered the room. Only then did he see an equally naked Martha sitting in one of the large soft chairs. She stood, and lifted her breasts with her hands and walked toward him.

"I talked Jenny into letting me stay. I figured that the three of us could have six times as much fun. It's been a long time since you took on two of us at once. Are you still man enough to handle us both?"

Kindermann laughed. Usually he didn't like surprises, but this one he did.

"Man enough? You're both going to regret those words before morning. Nobody is getting any sleep in here tonight!"

Morgan had left the big Concord stagecoach in Tucson. On the way there, Delsey had cuddled against him and slept part of the time. She pulled her jacket around her while it was dark and pressed his hand to her breast. It was covered, and the other passengers couldn't see. She mumbled something, and slept until they were almost into Tucson.

It had been an interesting trip. Delsey was not only beautiful, she was intelligent and quick as well. Her aunt in Phoenix ran a jewelry store. Her aunt's late husband had been the jeweler, but now she hired a jeweler and was doing well financially.

"So I'm sure my being there won't be a bother. I might even get to work in the store. I'd like that. Phoenix is growing. Some people think it will be the biggest place in the territory before long."

The ride had been long, and tiring. When they at last came to Tucson after dark, most of the passengers got off. Two more women got on board for the two-day ride on to Phoenix.

"If you come to Phoenix, you look me up," Delsey said. It was the best smile he'd ever seen. "The store name is the Johnson Jewelers. It's right downtown."

The driver motioned to Morgan, and he stepped back from the rig. Then the driver bellowed, the long leather reins slapped on horse's backs, and the rig jolted forward.

He watched it out of sight, then turned to the stage office. The rig on the way to Tombstone would be coming in some two hours later. Morgan sat outside in the cool of the Arizona evening and counted the stars. He wasn't nearly done when the stage arrived and Morgan got on board.

They would be in Tombstone about noon the next day, if Morgan could stand another battering, uncomfortable stage ride.

Slightly after noon the next day they did arrive in Tombstone. Morgan had slept by fits and starts along the way during the night, but he was still so tired he could barely move. He had visions of a big steak dinner at the hotel dining room, then about 24 hours of sleep in his room, and after that he would be ready to take on Kindermann, Sheriff Dirkin, and the Sutherland brothers all at once.

He stepped down from the stage and felt something jam into his side. Morgan turned, but a hand caught his jaw stopping him. Holding his face was one of the Sutherland brothers.

"Well, now, look who we found without a shotgun in his hands. Welcome back to Tombstone, Morgan. Fact is we've got such a stone all set aside for you.

Let's go measure the hole right now. I kind of want you to dig your own grave while I watch you. As you dig I'm gonna shoot you here and there in non-vital areas, just to watch you bleed!"

Chapter Nine

Buckskin Lee Morgan recognized the feel of a revolver barrel in his side. He glared at the shorter man in front of him holding a second six-gun an inch from Morgan's chest, and felt someone pull his Colt .45 from its leather.

"Slip right in here to the alley and we won't have so much company and such a big audience for you, Morgan," Sutherland said. "This is gonna pleasure me more than anything in months."

They pushed him toward the alley, and Morgan knew now wasn't the time to try to get away or he'd be dead, shot at least twice. They came to the alley mouth and walked inside, and Morgan stared at the short man beside him.

"Which one of the ugly Sutherland twins are you?"

A revolver barrel slammed into his left kidney, slightly from behind and just over his belt, and Morgan wanted to vomit. He swallowed hard, and then twice more before he could speak.

"Damn, Sutherland, but you are stupid. You don't even know how to hurt a man proper."

Morgan saw the blow coming this time, from the front and by the shorter Sutherland. He blocked it with his arm and jolted a straight right fist into the black-clad man's jaw. The Sutherland brother went down screaming in rage.

A moment later, a pistol butt came down on the side of Morgan's head and he never even felt it. That man knew what he was doing. Morgan slumped into the alley dirt and Sutherland swore.

"Damnit, Latigo, now we'll have to carry the big son of a bitch the rest of the way."

Latigo snorted, lifted Morgan to his back, and marched down the alley toward the residential street at the end. Roscoe Sutherland hurried to keep up, wiping a line of blood off his lips where the fist had bloodied his flesh against his teeth. At least no teeth were loosened or knocked out.

A buggy stood at the end of the alley. Morgan's hands were tied together and he was dumped in the rear section of the four-seater buggy. The other Sutherland brother, Nate, scowled as he saw Morgan was unconscious.

"How we gonna make him hurt if you've killed him already?" Nate asked.

"Ain't dead, just knocked out. Let's move. Drive this rig out of town before somebody sees us."

The three men and their victim rolled through two more residential streets, then across a low place, up a small hill, and then headed generally north for a mile before they stopped well out of Tombstone.

Morgan had come back to consciousness halfway along in the ride. He evaluated his situation without letting them know he was awake. Hands tied. Some big lug sitting in the rear buggy seat so he couldn't strangle one of the brothers from behind. His gun gone, and three to one against him, all three with revolvers at least.

Morgan remained limp when they lifted him from the buggy. It took two of them, and they strained to get his 185-pound body out of the buggy. Once they had him out, they dumped him on the ground and he let his head hit hard to prove he was still unconscious.

"Latigo, how the hell hard did you hit this bastard?" Nate asked the big man.

Morgan didn't hear a response. He opened one eye and saw the three standing near the buggy talking. There was a tree of sorts growing from the side of a wash where desert rains washed down the lowest runoff route dragging more sand and soil downstream to feed it. It was barely ten feet high and scraggly, not sturdy enough for a hanging. Good.

Morgan tried to think what he could do. His hands were tied tightly with two rawhide strips of leather. No chance to get them undone while the trio was watching.

The talk about digging a grave must have been wishful thinking, since they hadn't brought a shovel. What then? He still had his feet. He'd seen a Japanese man do terrible things to a gunman with a series of slashing kicks. Morgan didn't have the training, but one basic defensive tactic was available to him that he knew well. No, two. Kick and run.

A moment later the men came to him and the big man lifted him to his feet. One of the black-suited brothers slapped his face to bring him back to life.

Morgan made some growling motions and went limp again. One of the brothers stood directly in front of him. Out of slitted eyes Morgan judged the distance, sagged, then came up straight in a rush and kicked out as hard as he could with his right boot.

The hard leather grazed the side of the smaller man's inner thigh as it spread his legs, jolting upward. The hard leather top reached Nate Sutherland's crotch with lots of power left and smashed both of his testicles against his pelvic bones, crushing them, dropping Nate to the ground with a screaming roar of pain before he passed out from the intense, terrible agony.

Morgan wheeled at the same instant, ripping out of the big man's grasp behind him. He dropped down and grabbed the six-gun that Nate had carried, spun on his right foot the way he had seen the Oriental do, and slammed a spinning back kick against Latigo's chest. Latigo coughed and sank to his knees, drawing his Colt from leather.

Morgan dropped to one knee and, holding the borrowed revolver with both his tied hands, shot Latigo in the chest, blasting him backwards into the dust.

Another shot sounded close by and Morgan felt the sledgehammer blow as it hit him in the left shoulder and drove him back a step.

He turned, spotted the other Sutherland brother six feet away, and fired. His bullet cut through Roscoe Sutherland's chest, punctured the side of his lung, then slanted to the right and ripped into his heart, stopping the pump from working for eternity.

Roscoe jolted backwards three feet, slammed to the ground on his back, and never moved.

Morgan stared at the three men. Two of them had

to be dead, and the other Sutherland must wish he were. Morgan untied the leather thong from his wrists, then found his Colt .45 on the body of the big man and pushed it into leather. Then he dragged the two bodies to the buggy and lifted them in the back seat. He felt the pain in his shoulder, but it wasn't that intense. Blood dripped down his shirt and on the ground.

He picked up the unconscious Sutherland, then changed his mind and dropped him to the ground.

Let the little bastard get back to town on his own. Maybe Morgan could luck out and this Sutherland would die out there of exposure. Morgan drove the wagon back toward town. He used his kerchief to cover the wound in the back of his left shoulder, where he was sure there was a hole the size of a silver dollar.

He could still move his arm, and was thankful for that.

As he neared the downtown area he felt slightly woozy, and reached for the side of the buggy to steady himself. Then he looked down at the seat and saw that he was sitting in his own blood. He didn't know how much he had lost.

He was functioning on adrenaline and he didn't know how much longer that would keep him upright. He knew where one doctor's office was. Now he drove up the alley in back of it, left the buggy two doors down, and began the long walk, 50 feet to the medical man's rear door.

He leaned against a tree, then against a trash barrel, and at last made it to the door. He knocked, then tried the knob and opened the door.

A man looked at him. Morgan looked back and started to take a step into the hallway. He didn't make it. Before he could walk inside, the walls caved in and the roof fell down and somehow the floor rose to meet him all in the blink of an eye, and then he could see nothing but blackness.

A pounding came in his head. His back and shoulder burned like it was on fire. He flinched away from more pain.

"Damn, he's coming around. You got any of that sul ether?"

Something covered his face and the smell was terrible, then his very existence went black again.

Cold. Something felt wet and cold on his forehead. Someone held his hand. Voices sounded in the background but he couldn't hear what they said. Slowly he could understand.

"Is he coming around, Doctor?"

"Yes, yes. But remember, he lost a lot of blood. Nasty wound in his shoulder. Surprised he even got in here."

Morgan blinked open his eyes. It took him a moment to focus, then things cleared and he saw Miss Lily bending over him. Behind her was the chief of police, John Inman.

"Well, looks like he made it," Inman said. "Boy, you gave us some anxious moments there. You're not supposed to splash your own blood over half the county."

"Sorry," Morgan said. His voice sounded funny. He coughed and somebody drove needles into his shoulder. He couldn't keep the pain from his face.

"Lie still as you can, Morgan," said another man who leaned into Morgan's vision. "We ain't met, but I'm Doc Schroder. That shoulder is gonna hurt for a time, so stay in bed and don't move around much for at least a week. Now, the chief wants to ask you some questions."

"Morgan, it seems you left a trail of blood all the way from that buggy parked down the alley a ways right into this bed. That is your blood on the buggy seat isn't it?"

"Hard to tell, Chief."

"The two gents in the rear seat didn't bleed any. Leastways not in the buggy."

"If it was my blood on the buggy, Chief, what then?"

"Why, then I'd want to know how the two jaspers in the back seat came to meet their Redeemer."

"Odds are, Chief, in this town they got shot to death."

"Fact is that's what happened to them. What we need to know is who shot them and who shot you. Frankly, neither one of them is much of a loss to the community. But there are certain laws that have to be upheld."

"I'm all for that, Chief. Don't suppose you could get somebody to bring me a nice cold beer, could you? I have a strong urge for a cold beer."

Miss Lily stood up, patting his good shoulder. "I'll bring over a couple of mugs right away. Now don't you go running off."

When she left, the chief sat in the same chair. His voice dropped and he grinned.

"No need to play cat and mouse here, Morgan. I have two reports that the Sutherland brothers and the big ugly guy called Latigo kidnapped you off the street at the point of two guns. So can we say it was all a matter of self-defense? I'd be happy with that explanation and get the deaths written off my books and let you lay there and heal your shoulder."

Morgan eased his left arm an inch over on the white sheet, and the effort made him gasp and produced spots of sweat on his forehead.

"Course now, if it happened outside the city limits, that would be in the county sheriff's jurisdiction, and he might have a little different view on things, seeing he has that wanted poster on you for dead or alive."

Morgan tried to grin but it wouldn't quite work. "You're a hell of a lot smarter than I figured," Morgan said. "You're right, Chief. It happened inside the city limits. I kicked one of the boys in the crotch, put him down, got his gun, and the three of us shot it out. They lost, I won but paid a price."

"Where's the other one? The Sutherland with the smashed-up balls?"

"Out near the edge of town somewhere. Might even be county business unless somebody helps him back into town. North, out north somewhere. Follow the buggy tracks."

Chief Inman closed up the notebook he had been writing in and nodded at Morgan. "Now you better watch your hindside. Soon as Nate can talk he's gonna send six or eight gunmen after you. This is not a good spot to hide." The chief grinned, touched his hat, and walked out of the room.

Doctor Schroder looked in. "Mr. Morgan, would you like some laudanum to help kill that pain?"

Morgan shook his head. "Had a friend who got on that stuff when he was hurt, never could get off it. He finally bypassed the tincture and went straight to morphine. Said it was faster. He took too much one day and we buried him."

"Happens, sad to say."

Miss Lily came in with a fruit jar sealed tightly and a beer mug. She grinned and opened the fruit jar and poured the brew into the mug. It even foamed.

Two hours later, Morgan gritted his teeth as he walked across the street toward the Silver Queen. Wally, the apron from the Queen, had Morgan's right arm over his shoulder and was practically carrying Morgan.

For the past half block Morgan hadn't been able to talk as the pain drilled through him. Now he gasped as they pushed through the Silver Queen's doors.

"Guard's room," Miss Lily said softly, and soon he was lying in a bed, shivering and swearing softly.

Miss Lily sat in a chair beside him. She had a cold cloth on his forehead, and a full bottle of whiskey was on a small table. She poured a water glass full and lifted up his head so he could drink.

Morgan shook his head and sat up, wincing from the movement of his left arm.

"It didn't hurt this bad right after I was shot," Morgan said.

"The body can protect itself for a while. The doctors are starting to call the condition shock. The body kind of turns off the nerves in the affected area. A doctor in Denver told me about it once."

Morgan nodded and drank the rest of the whiskey. "One more glass should do it. Watch out for men from Nate Sutherland. He'll be out of his head with hatred."

Miss Lily's expression was serious. "I've hired two new guards to stand in the saloon with sawed-off shotguns ready at all times. Nobody would dare to try to come in here and find you."

"Let's hope. Pour me another glass."

It took Morgan two days to recuperate enough to get up and walk around and wear his .45. His left arm still didn't work right, and hurt every time he lifted it above his waist. But it was a pain he could live with.

It took Nate Sutherland two days to recover enough from his shattered testicles to be able to walk. The chief of police had found him the same day he was hurt, and taken the little man to Doc Schroder. There was no report made of the incident happening in county jurisdiction.

The morning of the third day, a small boy ran into the Silver Queen just before noon. He thrust a white envelope into Wally's hand as he stood at the end of the bar. Then the boy scurried out the door.

Wally stared at it a moment, then flagged down Morgan, who was taking exercise by walking up and down the saloon's length.

"Mr. Morgan. An envelope. I don't know what it says. It has writing on the front."

Morgan looked at it and saw his name and ripped it open. The note was short and to the point.

"Morgan. We have Miss Lily Larue. If you want her back without any injuries and alive, bring the grant deed to the Silver Queen and fifty thousand dollars. Get the money now, all in paper. We'll tell you where to deliver it. We'll send another envelope like this one to you there at the bar in three hours."

Morgan flexed his left hand and his left arm. It would have to do. It was time to get back to work.

Chapter Ten

They had kidnapped Miss Lily. There was only one thing Morgan could do: get ready to go after her. What would they expect? They would be watching the saloon. So he would go to the bank. He would take a small carpetbag with him, but he wouldn't put money in it. He came back from the bank after putting two newspapers in the carpetbag, then left again. This time he went out the back door of the saloon and down four doors to a hardware store.

There he bought ten sticks of dynamite, 20 detonator caps, and 20 feet of burning fuse. He put it all in the small carpetbag, and then walked down another half block in the alley to a lawyer's office he had noticed.

It took him ten minutes to get the lawyer to make up a fake grant deed. The lawyer said it was the kind that most of the property owners in town used. The four-page document was folded twice, and the front of it had green fancy printing on it and looked official.

With these items in hand, he went back to the saloon and checked his equipment. He cleaned and oiled his Colt .45, examined the sawed-off shotgun, and found a Winchester repeating rifle behind the bar. He cleaned and oiled it as well, and found 50 rounds for it. Morgan was going to be ready.

While he waited, Morgan paced the length of the room. At the same time he flexed his left hand and worked at raising it higher and higher. Gradually the pain eased and the muscles responded again.

He hated not being 100-percent fit when he had a job to do. Morgan decided that Nate Sutherland was behind the kidnapping, and that Nate would have two men helping him. Where? They would take Lily out of town. It would be easier to get the deed and then probably kill both Lily and Morgan.

Morgan was sure that Nate wanted to kill the man who'd killed his brother. He'd try for both in one play. Where would they take her? Not many places to hide in this country. No mountain cabins, no ranchers or small farmers. Maybe an abandoned mine along the San Pedro River somewhere. He'd know soon.

About two o'clock, three small boys rushed into the Silver Queen, eyes wide. They each carried a white envelope. They threw them on the bar, shrieked with excitement, and rushed out the front door.

Morgan checked the envelopes. One of them had a message inside. He read it carefully:

"Morgan. If you want to see Miss Lily alive, follow these directions to the letter. Bring no weapons.

Bring the grant deed for Miss Lily to sign and the $50,000 in greenbacks.

"Ride out the west road toward the river. Go about four miles to the river and turn upstream. You'll pass several mines in the hills along the river.

"After the third mine on the left you'll see a small feeder stream come into the San Pedro. It comes in from the right. Ride up that trail. There's a small abandoned mine about half a mile up the valley. As soon as you can see the mine, dismount and tie your horse and come on foot with the deed and the money.

"If you bring any weapons or if you try to attack us in any way, the woman will be killed at once and so will you. There will be six rifles aimed at you on your walk.

"Get on your horse now, and ride. Men will be watching you all along your trip."

The letter was not signed.

"Bad news, Mr. Morgan?" Wally asked.

"Tells me how to find Miss Lily. That's what I'm going to do. Don't worry. I won't let them hurt her, and they won't get the Silver Queen."

"Sutherland?"

"My guess. We'll both see you when we get back. You keep the place open here and use those two shotgun guards."

Morgan went out the front door to where he had tied his horse. He had rented a deep-chested black, a big sturdy mare who looked like she had staying power. He checked the sawed-off shotgun again and it just fit inside the carpetbag. He put another six-gun in there, the one he had taken away from Roscoe.

There would be no way he could conceal the Winchester. He'd have to make this a close-in war.

He checked his pockets again and found a packet of matches for the dynamite. He just hoped he had a chance to use it.

As he'd waited he had cut each stick of dynamite in half, and inserted a detonator and a six-inch length of burning fuse. The fuse was supposed to burn at a foot a minute, so six inches should last for 30 seconds. When he'd checked it without a detonator on the fuse, six inches of it had burned in about 20 seconds. Good enough.

Now he rode.

It was a cloudless sky and the sun burned down fiercely. By the weather it would be hard to tell if it were summer or winter. Actually it was July, the second hottest month of the year. Morgan moved along the trail toward the river and more of the mines. He turned upstream as instructed and counted the three mines on the left. When he saw the third one ahead he checked, and could see the small dry streambed angling off to the right.

He turned into the dry hills at once one ridge short of the designated path, and rode hard up the ravine. When he was a quarter mile into the hills, he climbed the slanting side of the slope to the ridgeline.

In the next small valley he spotted a run-down, abandoned try at silver mining. There were four buildings. One had a chimney and smoke came from it. The others were slightly larger. He saw four horses behind the occupied house. Four kidnappers, or three and Lily. Maybe one of them was down by the river watching.

He rode higher in the ravine until it petered out into another ridge. The black worked up and over the ridgeline. The hills there were barren, with a few sagebrush bushes, but mostly only sand, low-growing cactus, and a few weeds. No cover at all. He had to hope the kidnappers were all watching to the front.

He could see the old mine plainly now. He was a quarter of a mile behind it. He moved the horse back down the reverse slope and out of sight, then tied her to some greasewood. He took the carpetbag, made sure his six-gun was settled in leather, then hurried up and across the ridgeline and down toward the old mine.

About 50 yards down the slope, he found a small ravine that would give him cover from the mine. He worked down that and saw that it was the starting of the small valley that would open out below.

It shielded him for nearly 100 yards before it flattened out and he saw the first mine building less than 100 yards ahead of him. He went flat on his belly and didn't move. Reconnoitering time. He stared at the layout. The largest building was to the right. He could get at it from the rear and it had several holes in the wall where he could get inside.

What then? That would give him a look out the front at the other buildings. He moved slowly, cautiously, crawling over the sand and rocks to the right. He needed another 20 yards and then the big building would be directly in front of the smoking one, giving him cover.

A few minutes later he made it to the right spot, and stood and ran flat out for the side of the building. He made it puffing and his heart racing. His six-gun had been in his strong right hand all the way and the carpetbag in his left. There had been no angry rifle fire aimed at him. Maybe no one had seen him.

He tried to quiet his breathing and listened. There was only the sound of a soft breeze through the old frame structure. He checked both ways, then stepped inside the building through a hole in the wall.

It had been some kind of a barracks, with a few bunks still along the walls. He went across the creaking floorboards quickly to the far side, where a glassless window looked out on the rest of the mine site.

The building with smoke coming out of the chimney was in the best condition. It had a back door and one window, without glass, and he saw an outhouse to the right of it.

To the right sat another structure about the size of the one he was in. It had a large pair of doors halfway open that were hanging on tracks. To the left he could see the entrance to the mine and another small building. At first it looked like the mine shaft itself had been sealed, but he saw that though it was boarded up, it had a small man-sized door that stood open.

They wouldn't be in the mine, he told himself.

He watched and waited. He hadn't figured out any grand strategy. Rather he'd take it as it came, see what happened.

Fifteen minutes later the rear door of the building in front of him opened, and a man came out, looked around, stretched, adjusted the pistol in his holster, and walked to the outhouse. Morgan considered it. The window in the back of the occupied place stopped him. Otherwise he could have taken the man when he left the outhouse.

Instead Morgan watched the man go back into the house untouched. Four horses. If there were any lookouts down the trail they would have their horses with them. So it could be more than three men with Lily. He checked the sun. It was about four o'clock. There would be three hours of daylight yet, maybe more. He didn't want to wait that long for darkness.

There was no cover. No way he could get to that

back door and crash inside. Could he get to the horses? Yes, if he rushed to the next building on the right. Then, on the far side, he could see if there were any windows on the other side of the cabin. If not, he could get to the horses, untie them, and scare them into running. That might bring out one of the men.

He did it. A short run from the back of where he watched to the structure on the right and he was in position. Now he could see that the far side of the cabin had no window. He could get to the outhouse from there and the horses without being seen.

The screen door of the cabin banged again. A shorter man came out, stared around, looked at a pocket watch, and then walked to the outhouse.

Morgan grinned, and when the flimsy door closed on the one-holer, he ran for the side of the structure. Morgan went to the side so the door would open away from him. He took out his .45 Colt and held it by the barrel.

A minute later he heard a grunt inside the shack and a man backed out working at the buttons on his fly. Morgan slammed the Colt down hard. The butt hit the kidnapper squarely on top of his head and he sighed and crumpled to the ground. Morgan grabbed his shoulders and dragged him behind the outhouse. There he tied his hands and feet, and put his own bandanna over his mouth and knotted it in back as a gag.

One down. He stared at the horses. All were still saddled. Might as well. He hurried to them, untied the four reins from the hitching rail, and led all four horses along the side of the house. There he dropped the reins and whacked each mount with the butt of his Colt on their rear quarters, and they all loped away down past the cabin.

Morgan ran to the back side of the cabin and waited. Soon there was a yell from inside the cabin and a man ran out the rear door and charged down the slope after the horses. One of them stopped 50 yards down, but the other three kept running down the valley.

Another man came to the door, a six-gun in his hand. Morgan didn't recognize him. He shot him in the chest and the man slammed away from the door and lay still.

There was no sound from inside the cabin.

Hell, who wants to live forever, Morgan thought, and charged the back door. He got there alive, kicked the door open, and charged inside with his gun up, the carpetbag in the other hand.

Lily sat on the makeshift bed. She was bare to the waist. Lying on the bed was Nate Sutherland, naked and ready to make love. Lily jumped up and slapped Nate's erection, bringing a wail of pain from him, as he fumbled for a weapon. Lily smashed her fist down on his wrist just as he caught the six-gun. It clattered to the floor.

"What took you so long?" Lily asked, a big grin on her face.

"How many of them?" Morgan asked as he hurried to the bed and smashed his fist into Nate's jaw, jolting him back to the bed.

"Just the three. They figured that was plenty."

As she said it, a rifle round bored through the thin boards over the front windows and buried itself in the back wall.

"You inside, you're a dead man," someone outside called. "I've got six more men out here with rifles, so it's just a matter of time."

Morgan slid across the floor to the front door that had a hole in it and looked out. He saw the man 50 yards away behind some old ore cars. Out of range.

Lily ran over beside him. She hugged him and kissed his cheek. "It's a bluff. He doesn't have anyone but himself." They looked out the door again, then Lily turned.

"Nate's getting away!" she screeched.

Morgan turned. The naked man was almost out the door. Morgan tried to bring up his six-gun, but Lily turned at the same time and inadvertently knocked it out of his hand. By the time he picked it up and raced to the door, the starkly white naked man was out of pistol range. Nate ran 20 yards and through the open door into the mine tunnel.

Morgan gave Lily the shotgun and six extra shells. "Can you use this?"

She nodded.

"Watch out the front for that rifleman," Morgan said, and took the carpetbag and raced for the mine shaft. Twice the rifleman tried for him. After the first shot, Morgan heard the shotgun go off. Then the rifleman must have changed positions. The second round missed, and Morgan jolted to the ground behind some steel ore cars just in front of the open mine door.

He opened the carpetbag, tied two of the half sticks of dynamite together, and lit the fuse of one of them. When the fuse had burned down halfway, he threw the bomb in the open mine shaft door.

Five seconds later the powder exploded, sending a gush of dust and smoke out the small door and slamming a blast back the other way into the tunnel.

Morgan waited until the smoke and dust cleared.

"You want to come out peaceable, Nate?" Morgan called in the door.

There was no response. The rifleman 75 yards below sent a round slamming into the metal ore car, and Morgan ducked back behind it.

Two minutes later the dust was gone and Morgan dashed into the mine tunnel before the shooter below could fire. He paused to let his eyes adjust to the darkness. The sunlight shone through the open door, making the first 20 feet of the tunnel light as day.

Morgan saw no one in that area.

"Nate, you might as well come out and give up. There's nowhere to go back there and you know it. Just a bunch of side tunnels and maybe a deep shaft or two that you just might fall into."

A derringer blasted from 20 feet away in the edge of the darkness.

"Hell, Morgan, I'm not dead yet. But you're going to be. Told you I have six more men out there."

"Your bluff won't work, Nate. One of your men is dead, the other one tied up, and Lily has a shotgun holding off the third. That's your team. Give it up."

Morgan moved as soon as he spoke, and the derringer fired again at the spot where he had been.

"Now you have to reload, Nate," Morgan said, and rushed forward into the blackness. He paused just inside the dark and listened. Footsteps slapped the hard tunnel floor ahead as Nate ran deeper into the coal black tunnel.

Morgan moved slower now. He wished he had something to make a torch of. The fake deed. He took it out, twisted it as tightly as he could, and lit it with a match from his pocket. It flared up and he could see for a moment. Then at the side of the tunnel he saw one of the torches that had been placed there long ago by the diggers.

They were rags wrapped around a pole and probably soaked with kerosene. He pulled one down and lit it. Most of the kerosene had evaporated, but there was enough to make a good burning light.

Morgan moved forward quicker now, and heard the running steps again. Then there was the sound of breaking wood followed by a wail and a scream, then only silence.

Chapter Eleven

Buckskin Lee Morgan held the torch low now as he worked slowly forward along the old silver mine tunnel. He could see Sutherland's footprints in the inch-deep dust on the floor of the long-unused tunnel. Somewhere ahead Sutherland must have fallen.

Fifty feet on down the tunnel he found a broken barrier. It was a wooden fence around a shaft that had been sunk straight down in the tunnel. The near side of the wooden fence had been broken and smashed inward. Part of it hung down in the darkness of the shaft.

Morgan held the torch down as far as he could reach, but he couldn't see the bottom. He took a section of the broken board. It was jagged and caught fire quickly from the torch. When it blazed up well he held it over the shaft, then dropped it.

Morgan watched it fall down and down. At last the wind of the plunging board blew out the flames. It was several seconds later before he heard the board hit the bottom.

"Sutherland, are you down there?" Morgan called. There was no response. Could the little man have faked it? Morgan checked the tracks again. They came directly to the wood, then there were skid and sliding marks in the thick dust and then the hole. He walked all the way around the shaft using the torch to examine the inch-thick dust. Nowhere did he find any footprints laid down by Nate Sutherland.

Until the sheriff lowered a pair of lanterns down the hole without finding a body, Morgan would consider the second Sutherland brother out of business.

He went back to the tunnel opening, and heard the shotgun fire from the cabin. A moment later he saw the rifleman run and catch one of the horses, step into the saddle, and ride down the valley toward the river.

Morgan ran to find Miss Lily. She had dressed and combed her hair.

"By your expression, I'd say that we don't have to worry about the last Sutherland brother anymore. Right?"

"Right," Morgan said.

They rode into Tombstone just before dark. Morgan had picked up his horse, then untied the man behind the outhouse and told him to ride out of the territory if he didn't want to answer to a kidnapping charge.

Wally grinned when they came in the Silver Queen.

"Good to have you back, Miss Lily," he said.

"Good to be back. Anything happen while we were gone?"

"Not much. Oh, Sheriff Dirkin was in and said he'd like to see Mr. Morgan. He didn't say what about."

"That's not good news, Lee Morgan," Lily said. "Don't go over there and see him."

"Not likely. He must have found that wanted on me."

"So what will you do?"

"Have a friendly discussion on neutral ground. Maybe in the chief of police's office. The fact is that the sheriff had no jurisdiction where the shooting took place. It happened within the city limits, and the chief of police at the time said it was self-defense. That should have ended it."

There was a commotion at the front door, and shortly two men came walking in. Lily stood up at once directly in front of Morgan.

"Well, if it isn't Senator Latimore Potts. What brings you into my small little piece of the world?"

"Well, Miss Lily herself. How is Tombstone's prettiest whore?"

"At least I give honest service for what I get paid for. Not like some slimy politician who constantly tries to find new ways to steal the people of the territory blind."

Latimore Potts had come to within a dozen feet of Lily, and now he bristled with fury. Potts was five-eight, clean-shaven, with bulging eyes and a high forehead. He had massive arms and was built square like a brick pillar.

"You calling me a thief in front of all these witnesses?" he thundered.

"Hey, I just said politicians do that. If the shoe fits,

Senator, you can stuff it on your foot and then in your mouth."

Potts took two steps toward Lily, but Morgan jumped up and moved in front of her.

"You have a problem, Potts?" Morgan asked, with a deadly tone that at once quieted the whole saloon.

"Who the hell are you?" Potts asked.

"Who the hell do you think you are, barging in here and insulting this lady? I should teach you some manners."

Potts stepped back as if he had been struck. "Nobody talks to me that way in my town."

"So you bought this town and paid for it, right, Senator? You'd do better to tend to the business of the territory, not your own pockets and bank account."

"Don't I know you?"

"Not if your slime rubs off on me you don't."

"You're Morgan, right? The bastard who shot my kid brother in the back and then shot him twice more to make sure he was dead."

"Is that Chief Inman there?" Morgan asked.

"Yes, I'm here."

"Chief, you're my witness. This man who calls himself Potts just slandered me in front of fifty witnesses. I want to bring a charge of slander against him. I trust you'll write up the charges and present them to the court."

"Absolutely, I'll do that. Such is part of my job as chief of police in my jurisdiction, which is the city of Tombstone."

Potts took a step forward. "Slander? Impossible, Morgan. Everything I said is true and you know it. Therefore, Morgan, I'm taking you in for the murder of my brother. I'm acting on the wanted poster in the sheriff's office of this county."

"Potts, that poster is nothing more than a private printing," Morgan said. "It's worthless. I have the witnesses and the city police chief's statements to prove that it's also untrue. Besides, the incident took place in city jurisdiction, not county. Therefore the county sheriff had no right to bring the charges or cause the poster to be printed."

"Shut up, killer!" Potts roared. "Chief, I order you to arrest that man and jail him on the murder charges brought by the wanted poster."

Chief Inman drew himself up as tall as he could and glared at the accuser. "Senator, you might be a big son of a bitch in Phoenix, but back home here, you're just one more voter. You try ordering me around again and I'll throw you in jail for disturbing the peace. Do I make myself clear?"

"But that man's a—"

"Quiet!" Inman roared. "Morgan was completely cleared of any charges before he left town. You were in Phoenix when it all happened four years ago. I figured you'd be in town here sooner or later, so I looked back in the files and found the case you refer to. Now don't move, I'm going to read this report.

"It's dated April 15, 1879. On this date one Wilfred Potts was shot dead in a saloon by one Buckskin Lee Morgan. The incident began when Potts stumbled and fell against Morgan at a poker table. Potts said Morgan tripped him and demanded to fight. In the ensuing conversation, Potts, who was near falling-down drunk, swore at Morgan and ended by falling across the poker table, ending the game, breaking the table, and unseating Morgan.

"Potts regained his feet and demanded that they settle the problem with a shoot-out. Potts was so drunk he could hardly stand.

"Morgan told him to go home and sober up. Friends took Potts away, but later he returned and demanded satisfaction from Morgan. Potts stood at one end of the bar and began his draw. He was so slow that Morgan waited for him. At last Morgan shot Potts in the right shoulder and he went down.

"Potts held onto his six-gun and fired at Morgan, missing by three feet on one side. The next shot was that much wide on the other side. Morgan then fired, hitting Potts in the left shoulder. Potts got his bearings and aimed again. Morgan fired one last shot in self-defense to save his life and killed Potts.

"This report concludes that Morgan acted humanely, tried to get Potts to stop several times, gave him every advantage, and at last had to kill Potts before Potts killed him. This case details the classic definition of self-defense and no charges can or should be brought in this situation. This case is closed."

Chief Inman looked up. "Potts, your late brother was a no-good drunk who couldn't hold a job, who nearly drank himself to death, and in the end caused his own demise. If you have any quarrel with that, you take it up with the Attorney General of the Territory."

Half of the men in the saloon clapped and hooted when Potts tried to talk. At last he turned, red-faced and furious, and stormed out of the saloon.

"Another friend made," Morgan said softly. Miss Lily snorted, then took his arm and led him back to his guard's room near the back of the saloon beyond the girls' dining room.

"So do you think the problem of the wanted posters is finished?" Lily said.

"Maybe, maybe not. Even if the new sheriff sent out a recall letter on all of those posters, it's hard to tell where they might have been sent, and where they might have been passed around and carried by bounty hunters. I'll probably have trouble with that poster for another fifteen years."

"At least you settled the problem of the Sutherland brothers—settled *my* problem, that is."

"They came after me, I didn't go after them."

"So what else is on your list of projects to do?"

"Remember Taft Tambert?"

"Yes, the man who is missing out at the Silver Nugget."

"He is missing, but he's also dead. I made a promise to his wife that I'd find out what I could about how he died and who killed him. That's next on my agenda."

"Kindermann is no Latimore Potts. Potts is mostly bluster and fakery. Kindermann is practical, and I've heard he runs his place with an iron hand."

"He also kills people. I have a lot of trouble with that kind of guy running around loose."

"So you aim to cinch up his straps a little."

"More or less, after it gets dark enough."

"A word of warning. I know you're good with your gun, but out there at the mine the guards shoot first and then find out who they killed. I used to know one of the night guards and they don't take any chances."

"Thanks, that's good to know. Well, looks like it's dark enough outside."

"No rest at all? Damn. I figured maybe we could do a little resting and holding. I haven't even thanked you for saving me up there. They were all set to steal the Silver Queen back and kill both you and me."

"I figured that."

Morgan had sent for his gear from the hotel when he got shot. Now he took out a black, long-sleeved shirt and pulled it on. He looked at his pants and decided they were dark enough. He strapped on his .45, put six of the half sticks of dynamite inside a dark jacket pocket, and was ready.

Miss Lily trailed one finger down his jaw, then kissed his lips and pulled back. "Be careful and good luck," she said. Then he slipped out the alley door heading for the Silver Nugget. The mine was three miles from the town, and he rode the same black he had used that afternoon. He left her when he could see the lights at the tunnel head. He put her in a little low spot where she couldn't be seen from the main trail, then hiked around to the back of the mine and lay in the dirt and rocks watching the Silver Nugget layout.

The night shift had gone into the hole. Ore cars came out from the tunnels to the stamping plant. It all looked like a normal mine operation. The reduction facility was what he needed.

He would become a guard. It took him two hours of watching to determine where the watchmen were and what posts they walked or stood. He picked the one who walked around the back of the reduction plant. That one was out of sight of the other guards for more than ten minutes on his rounds.

Morgan moved through the night like a shadow, not making a sound, not casting any unnatural shapes in the moonlight. He wished for some trees and shrubs or big rocks or some cover, but there was none. He crouched curled around rock for five minutes as the guard marched his way past an open area.

Then Morgan worked his way silently down a gully in back of the building to a spot where the guard would pass. When the man made his next pass, Morgan came up just behind him and hit him on the head with his .45, and the guard went down in a heap.

Morgan slipped off the man's light jacket, which

seemed to be his badge of office—all the guards had them—and put on the hat with the bill on the front. He dragged the guard back well out of sight. He tied up the man, put a gag in his mouth, picked up the Winchester repeater, and hurried away.

Morgan first went to the small back door in the building and found it locked. He moved on to the next door and it was open. Morgan slipped through the door, turned his back, and closed it and locked it with a bolt. He had been aware that there were lights on in the big building. It had several rooms, and the one he was now was filled with large vats 20 feet square. He couldn't tell how deep they were. The smell was almost overwhelming. He walked along the side of the vats to a stairway, and went up it and into a smaller room. It was filled with pipes and gauges with one man watching them.

The man nodded and Morgan continued on through to another room. This one had what appeared to be furnaces of some sort, but now they were cold. At once he recognized a smelting operation, where the silver evidently was melted down into ingots. The final product.

One man sat at a bench working over a ledger. He looked up and frowned. "Hey, guard. What the hell you doing in here?"

"Ain't I supposed to be here? My first night on the job. Hell, they said to come here. This is the reduction plant, right?"

"Yeah, but you're supposed to be outside. Marching around on the outside, damnit!"

Morgan walked closer to him. "Oh, well, then I guess they changed the orders. You the boss here?"

The man laughed. "Hell, no, I'm just the tally man."

"Oh, the job that Taft Tambert used to have before he vanished."

"Yeah, right, so what?"

Morgan's .45 came out of leather in an eye blink. He pushed it hard into the soft flesh under the tally man's chin.

"Just so there's no doubt about what's going on here, I'll blow your head off in a second if I think you're lying to me or not helping me enough, understand?"

The tally man's eyes went wide, his chin quivering in panic. "Yeah, sure. I don't know much."

"Where is the silver kept, the bars of silver?"

"Over there in the big vault. It's got a lock on it that only Mr. Kindermann can open. Only him."

"Where's the rest of the silver?"

"What do you mean? It's kept in the vault."

"All of it?" Morgan asked, and pushed harder with the .45 muzzle. "Remember, no lies or you're a corpse. Then all of your saved money won't do you no good."

Morgan repeated the question.

"No, no, you're right not all the silver is kept in the vault."

"Yeah!" Morgan said softly. "Now we're getting somewhere."

Chapter Twelve

"Move the damn gun and I'll tell you where the silver is," the tally man said.

Morgan pulled it down and punched it hard into the tally man's belly. "You ever been gut-shot? Ever seen a man gut-shot? He always dies, but sometimes slower than other times. An hour at the least, maybe two hours at the most, of the most awful pain a human can stand. Not enough to make you pass out, just leave you in agony, then finito."

"Okay, okay, I get the picture. I'll make you a partner. Kindermann has stolen lots of silver. The two of us will get the silver tonight and take it out of here. Then we split fifty-fifty, right?"

"Maybe. First, how do I know you can get us to the silver?"

"Because I help the old man hide it every time we

cast. We send the rest of the men to other jobs and then we take a cartload of silver to another tunnel that nobody knows about."

"Nobody but you and Kindermann?"

"Right! There must be a hundred bars in there by now. Twenty pounds each. That makes a ton of silver! How much is that worth?"

"More than both of us could spend in a lifetime. But how do we transport a ton of silver out of here without every guard in the place shooting us full of holes?"

"Damn easy. I'm one of the guards most times. I just tell them we're moving some chemicals for the reduction plant that just arrived. These dumb galoots won't know the difference."

"You're serious about this?" Morgan asked.

"Damn right! I don't owe Kindermann a thing. He's probably getting ready to dump me down a mine shaft the way he did the other tally men. I promised myself I'd get out of here before he killed me. Now's the time. Come on."

Morgan followed the lanky youth, who couldn't be more than 22 or 23, down to the melting room and along the back side of the building behind the furnace to a set of double doors.

"That's where the vault is with most of the silver. We can't get at that, but on down here . . ."

They went to the end of the building to a battered wall that had a ragged door on it. The kid opened the door, swinging it on rusty hinges. Behind it was the face of the mountain and an old tunnel. It looked unused. Then Morgan saw by the light of the lanterns they carried that the floor of the tunnel had been tramped down by many boot marks.

The kid hurried along and showed where a room had been carved out that now contained a stack of 20-pound silver bars.

"Told you there must be a hundred," the kid said. "Now do you believe me? Kindermann is taking a percentage—about twenty percent, I'd guess—of the production. Then reporting the rest of it to his stockholders and backers in Phoenix."

Morgan picked up one of the bars and cut it with his knife. Silver all the way through. "Now, how do we get this out of here?"

"I've been working on that plan for two weeks. I can get a team and a wagon. I tell the guards outside I have to bring in some new chemicals for the vats. I cover them up and bring them in. We unload them, load on the silver, and drive out with the guards expecting us."

"Could work."

"It will. First we get rid of your guard shirt and the rifle. That would be a giveaway. Then you stay here out of sight while I go get the wagon and the chemicals. They run short from time to time, so this happens now and then. Most of the guards have seen it done. But they aren't allowed inside the building. Down there's a big door. We drive the wagon and team right inside."

"When we get outside, what happens?"

"We drive toward the river and tell the guards we're going to town for an emergency shipment of chemicals that came in on the freight wagon. They never will bring them out here. I took one other trip at night to get them when we ran out. So it's unusual but has happened before. We'll keep the silver flat on the bed of the wagon covered by tarps and blankets that will supposedly cushion the bottles of chemicals."

Morgan debated it. The whole setup made sense. If he could get this silver out of here, he'd have proof for the partners in Phoenix that Kindermann was cheating them. They'd sack him.

"Let's do it. Move fast, we don't have much time. What's your name?"

"Lenny. Who are you?"

"Morgan."

Lenny moved to the old door. "This door doesn't have a lock on it, and I can't lock you in. Just let me close it most of the way so it'll look normal. I've got the wagon all set, but it'll take me about twenty minutes to get the bottles on it and drive in here. You watch for me."

Lenny ran out and swung the heavy door almost closed. Morgan pushed a rock in the way so it couldn't close all the way. Then he waited. He checked by the lantern light on his pocket watch. There was a chance the kid was double-crossing him, but Morgan didn't think so. He'd had a plan all worked out to steal the goods, a good plan.

He'd be back.

Twenty-five minutes after he left, Lenny was back. A big door creaked open 50 feet away in the building and a team and wagon drove in. Lenny thanked the guards, who closed the door.

It took Morgan and Lenny a half hour to load the 96 bars of silver in the wagon. They carried four bars on each trip at first, then three on each trip. They laid the bars side by side in the bottom of the wagon, and put canvas and old blankets over them and empty chemical bottles. Then Lenny pushed the door open and they drove out. He jumped down and closed the door. One guard looked at them and shrugged and continued on walking his assigned post.

"Now is the hard part," Lenny said. "We have to cross another line of guards just beyond the main office building. One of them will be the night guard lieutenant, and he isn't too easy to fool. I know him."

They came along the dirt track to the spot and two guards ran out of the darkness. One was the night lieutenant. He looked at Lenny.

"Lenny, I heard you were moving some chemicals tonight."

"Bloody well going to charge the boss extra pay. Work half the day and then all fucking night. I'm as pissed off as hell. Now we got to drive all the way to Tombstone and bring back some fucking chemicals so they don't run out. How about me and you trading places for this run, Lieutenant?"

The man laughed and shook his head. "Not a chance. Looks like your helper there is half asleep already."

"Never could get good help. I even promised him the name of my girl in town, but he wanted money."

"My kind of man," the guard lieutenant said, and waved them on through.

Neither Morgan nor Lenny spoke for a minute.

"Now what can we do with it?" Morgan asked. "The old man will be out of his mind when he finds this silver gone."

"I was planning on hiding it in an old unused mine nearby," Lenny said.

"So you would have to stay there and guard it, and when Kindermann came with ten riflemen searching every old mine in the area, you'd be a new kind of sieve from all the bullet holes in you."

"So where do we take it?"

"I know just the spot. We drive to Tombstone. Oh, just in case you get greedy, I'll have my six-gun on you the rest of the way, so drive nicely and you'll get two bars. That's a thousand dollars or more. Should keep you going for some time."

Lenny wilted a little. Then he grinned. "Hell, I didn't know how I was going to turn all that silver into cash anyway. It's stamped with the maker and the date."

"Carve that much off and cut it up with an axe," Morgan said. "Sell it to a jeweler, or melt it down into smaller bars. A good blowtorch will melt it."

"What you doing with the rest?"

"Giving it back to the folks who own it, except for a few bars for Ted Tambert's wife Delsey. Kindermann owes her that. I'll contact his backers in Phoenix and turn it over to them when they come out here to fire Kindermann."

Lenny laughed. "Well, I guess some good will come out of all this after all. Just wonder how much longer I had before Kindermann killed me. Not long, I'll wager. Where we hiding the silver, in a bank somewhere?"

"Safer than that," Morgan said. "You'll be surprised. No, better you don't know. You have any cash money?"

"Cash? Why?"

"When we hit Tombstone, you'll need to chop up your two bars of silver so they'll fit into a saddlebag. Then you'll need to buy a horse and saddle so you can ride for Phoenix or St. Louis or wherever you're going. That means getting gone tonight."

"I carry my bank on me. Yeah, I got some cash, near three hundred."

"Good, I'll drop you off at the livery stables."

An hour later, the heavily laden wagon let Lenny off at the livery and Morgan made sure he wasn't followed. Then he drove to the alley behind the Silver Queen and pounded on the door until Lily came to open it.

Morgan didn't say a word, he just started carrying

silver bars into the guard's room where he had been sleeping. He stacked them under the bed, made sure the floor boards would hold, then put more down, and when he had them all there he covered them with a blanket and sat down and wiped the sweat off his forehead.

"You're stealing silver bars now, Morgan?" Lily asked.

"Kindermann stole them first. I just took them from him. Some of them go to the widow Tambert, I get two of the beauties, and the rest go back to the partners in the Silver Nugget who will be storming in here from Phoenix as soon as I can get off letters to them."

"Sounds like you put in a good night's work."

"I keep trying."

"What's all that silver worth?"

"Not sure. My guess about five hundred dollars a bar. That times ninety bars would be about forty-five thousand dollars."

Lily shook him where he sat dozing off on the bed. "I'd suggest going to bed, but first you've got to move that team and wagon. Kindermann is going to be all over town soon enough. We don't want him panting right up to my door."

Morgan nodded, went back out, and drove the team to the far side of town and left them. Someone would find them in the morning. He walked back and into the rear door of the bordello, barred it, and fell on his bed. He had barely touched the pillow when he went to sleep. An hour later he woke up when he tried to turn over. That was when he took off his shirt and his gun belt, but he kept the loaded .45 Colt near his pillow.

The girls' chatter awoke him the next morning. It was ten minutes to noon when he pulled on a clean shirt and washed his face. He shaved in cold water, working carefully with a just-stropped razor.

He didn't have to tell Lily not to mention the treasure hiding under his bed. Now he wondered how soon Kindermann would discover his loss. Morgan figured it would be this morning, early probably, as soon as the guards reported the wagon that had left and the failure of it to return with the tally man. Kindermann would know at once even before he checked the tunnel.

He could be on his way to town right now. Fine. He didn't know Morgan. Lenny should be well on his way to Tucson. There was no way Kindermann could tie Morgan into the missing silver.

Morgan had a quick breakfast just as the girls were leaving. Then he went and talked to the banker to see if he knew who Kindermann's backers in Phoenix were.

The banker was quite helpful. He named three of them and gave Morgan their addresses. An hour later Morgan had written letters to the three, detailing how Kindermann was stealing 20 percent of the silver production before reporting it to the partners. He said he was a friend who thought they would like to know. The silver had been kept in a secret unused tunnel next to the reduction building.

The letters would go out on the morning stage to Phoenix.

Morgan had just settled down in a chair in the sun in front of Bauer's Market on Fremont Street when he saw a familiar form marching down the boardwalk. He looked again, and as the man came closer, Morgan was sure of it.

He jumped to his feet and moved to meet the man.

"Good afternoon, Mr. Roustenhauser. I was just

about to send you a wire. I think I've found your missing daughter, Hortense."

Roustenhauser preened his mustache and muttonchops.

"Well, it's about damn well time. Take me to her right now."

Chapter Thirteen

Morgan looked at the smaller man in surprise and shook his head. "I'm sorry, Mr. Roustenhauser, but I can't take you to your daughter without any warning. You know how women are. She hasn't seen you for what, three years? You can't just pop in and surprise her. I'm sure she'll want to get her hair fixed and get dressed up. You know how women are.

"Tell me where you're staying and I'll go see her and set up a meeting. I'm sure she's just as anxious to see you as you are to see her."

"Damn unusual. I've just traveled for a week and a half to get here and now I have to wait?"

"Sir, I see that you're all shaved and combed and have on a proper suit and all. Don't you think that Hortense deserves to have the same right to look her best when she meets you again?"

"All right, all right. But I don't plan on being in town for any longer than I have to. This is a terrible place, and the weather is the worst I've ever seen."

"You're staying at the Hanover House?"

"Yes, terrible little hotel, but the best one."

"Fine, I'll go see Miss Hortense and give her the glad news. Then I'll tell her that you want to see her just as soon as possible." Morgan nodded and walked away rapidly. He didn't need a complication like this. Kindermann would be in town at any minute and Morgan had to be ready to make adjustments and change any plans until his letters could bring the partners from Phoenix. Most important, he had to protect that silver. The partners couldn't get here from Phoenix for at least six days at the minimum. Damn!

Morgan figured that the brewmaster was watching him as he walked away, so he turned in at the hardware store, went out the back door to the alley, and then down to the Silver Queen Saloon. He grabbed Miss Lily by the hand and tugged her into his room in back on the first floor.

"You've got problems," he said when the door closed behind them.

"What on earth . . ."

"Your father is in town."

"My father?"

"Yes. Hans Roustenhauser is staying at Hanover House. He knows you're in town and he's come here to find you."

Her face went white and she sat down quickly on his bed.

"How did he know—? First, how did you know who I am? I'm not going to budge until you tell me. The truth, damnit, Morgan, the plain honest truth for a change."

He told her quickly, straight, holding her hands as

he did so she couldn't hit him. When he finished she reached in and kissed his cheek.

"Dear, sweet Lee Morgan. Thank you for being so considerate. You could have told him I was here that first night, demanded your pay, and left town."

"I wouldn't do that to you."

"Hey, I'm just another whore."

He put his fingers over her lips. "Never again are you going to say that. We have about an hour or two at the most for you to get your story ready. We'll have the meeting in that fancy restaurant, the Top Sirloin. You wear your most conservative dress." He stopped. "You do want to see him, don't you?"

"Yes, he's still my father."

"And you do want to go back to Denver?"

"I . . . I don't know. I guess it depends how Father treats me. I have to have my freedom. I want some job I can work at where I can use what I've learned here."

She flashed him a smile. "No, I don't want to open a bordello in Denver. Something a little classier than that. A woman's high-class dress shop, maybe. Father has the money to get me started."

She lifted her brows. "That might be nice. Yes, I'll think about that. All right. I'll change clothes, wash the rouge off my lips and cheeks, and be Daddy's little girl one more time. But we're going to have an open and frank discussion. Oh, does he know what I've been doing, about the Silver Queen?"

Lily looked at him. "Did you tell him . . . what I'm doing here, how I've made my living the past three years?"

"Of course not."

"Good, then I get to. At which time he'll probably throw me out of the restaurant, disinherit me, and rush back to Denver." She stared, her gaze traveling far off. "Denver isn't so bad. Maybe I could learn to ice skate and get a toboggan."

"I'll go tell your father where we'll meet. What time?"

"Four o'clock. That will give me time to get my mind and my vocabulary ready for dear Father."

"Don't be too hard on him."

Lily giggled. "Don't say hard-on around a . . . a former lady of the evening."

Morgan took a swipe at her bottom and hurried out of the room.

He found Roustenhauser pacing the boardwalk in front of the Hanover House hotel. The man didn't look as imposing now with worry and a little bit of tiredness showing.

They made the appointment, and Morgan pointed out the Top Sirloin Restaurant half a block down the street. Then Morgan walked down a half block the other way and watched the street. He hadn't heard any gunfire. Maybe Kindermann wasn't in town yet. He'd give a hundred dollars to watch when Kindermann discovered that his stolen silver had been stolen in return.

Morgan watched the streets for another hour, then went to pick up Lily and take her to the meeting. He'd drop her at her father's table, say a quick hello, and then leave. That was the plan.

Lily was ready and waiting when he got back to the Silver Queen. They went out the door, and he was pleasantly surprised by her dress. It was old-maid modest, covered her from chin to neck to shoe sole, and showed nothing of her fine figure. Her face had been washed clean and held no rouge or lip paint at all.

It brought out her natural beauty, and her light blue eyes sparkled against her freshly washed and combed blonde hair.

"You look like a princess this afternoon," Morgan

said. She held his arm lightly, her hat crowding down on her face to shield it.

"I'm trying so hard," she said. Lily grinned. "So far not one swear word or dirty phrase. I'm doing better. Are you sure I look all right?"

"You'll look so good to your father he'll be sure to ask you to come back. He'll probably put a story in the Denver *Rocky Mountain News* that you've been in Switzerland going to school."

She laughed, and it drained away some of the tenseness he could feel through her arm.

"Relax, it's going to be fine. It will all work out well."

"If it doesn't I can always take your ton of silver and run for Mexico."

"True, you could, but you won't."

"What I can't figure out is why you're giving most of it back."

"It's honest earned silver. The partners in Phoenix don't know anything about Kindermann's crooked little scheme. He must have done this before, selling the silver for himself. At least this part will go back to the people who invested their money to mine it. Except for a couple of the bars for Delsey Tambert and for me."

"If it had been Kindermann's silver?"

"If that bastard had owned it outright, I'd have taken the whole ton and laughed over his grave."

They were at the restaurant. Morgan handed her in the door, then looked over the diners in the large room. Each table had a linen cloth over it.

Roustenhauser stood up at a table near the door, and Morgan piloted Lily through the chairs to the table.

Morgan looked at them both. "You two have a good talk. I have an important meeting."

Lily grabbed his arm. "No, Morgan, I want you to

stay here. I have no secrets from Mr. Morgan. That will be all right, won't it, Father?"

Roustenhauser lifted his brows. Morgan guessed he was seeing a strong woman for the first time, and not the little girl who had left home.

"Well, certainly, certainly, sit down. I've already ordered."

"Call the waiter, Father, I'll order for myself. But thank you for the kindness."

They sat down.

"You're looking well, Hortense," her father said.

"I'm feeling just fine, Father. You look well yourself."

The waiter brought coffee for all of them, and they didn't talk until he had left.

Mr. Roustenhauser sipped his coffee and looked at his daughter. Then he scowled at Morgan. "Mr. Morgan, I've changed my mind. You will leave now, please. I can't talk freely with you here."

Morgan started to stand, but Lily's hand on his arm stopped him.

"Father, I know this is hard for you, but if Mr. Morgan leaves, then I do as well. I'm a grown woman now, and I don't need a lecture and a scolding by my father."

"That isn't what I'm planning on talking about!" Roustenhauser said, his voice rising. People at the next table turned and looked at him. He took a long breath and tears nearly overflowed his eyes. He beat back his emotions.

"Maybe it would be best if I did leave," Morgan said. "This is a private family talk." He stood.

"No!" Lily shouted. More heads in the restaurant turned.

"Very well," Roustenhauser said. He stood, turned, and was gone before Morgan could say a word.

"Oh, damn!" Lily said softly. "Get me out of here."

Morgan dropped two quarters on the table, paying more than the coffee would cost, and they left by the side door.

"Christ, I guess I really botched that situation. What the hell should I do now?"

Morgan looked at Lily, who stood close to him on the boardwalk. He took her arm and urged her down the street. They went around the block and up the alley to the Silver Queen. "The first thing we do is get you settled down. The second is for me to give you a scolding. The next time we get a meeting with your father, I won't even be there. But you will stay and you will talk with the man. He spent two weeks traveling to get here to find you. Give him a little bit of slack on the reins."

Lily pushed her head against his chest and closed her eyes.

"You're right. Okay, the next time I'll let Father have his way and let him talk. But then I may have to do some talking as well."

"Good, talking is the way to start to solve problems. Now, let me get out of here and try to set up another meeting tonight, but in another public place. Maybe the lobby of the Hanover House. There are those two soft chairs over on the side."

"I know the spot. Fine with me if you can talk to him. Sometimes Daddy wouldn't talk to me for days at a time."

"Have you figured out what you're going to do?"

She looked at him, then at the front of the saloon, then up the stairs and back down. Slowly she shook her head. "No, not really. Oh, it would be good to go home. No more money worries, no saloon to run, no women to keep from clawing each other to pieces, no drunks to handle.

"But then I'd be Daddy's little girl again and have to do what he said and be nice to his friends, and it would end up being the whole damn thing all over again."

"Not necessarily. There are things to do in Denver, positions a woman with your business talents might investigate. And if you sell the Silver Queen you'd have another ten or fifteen thousand dollars, plus what you have already there in the bank. Something to think about."

"I've thought about it . . . a little dress shop, fancy clothes, expensive, well made. I don't know."

"You keep thinking while I go and see if I can talk to your pa."

Lily laughed. "Nobody ever called my father Pa before. Good luck."

A half hour later, Morgan decided he needed more than good luck. He had found Roustenhauser's room number at the desk of the Hanover House hotel, but the man wouldn't answer his knock.

Morgan tried for ten minutes, at last shouting at the man that he was acting like a little boy who didn't get to eat the whole gooseberry pie. Morgan stormed off as angry as he had been in weeks.

He sat in the lobby for the rest of the afternoon and until ten o'clock at night. Roustenhauser did not come through the lobby or go to the dining room. The old boy must have been getting hungry by then.

Morgan reported back to the Silver Queen, and told Lily that he hadn't been able to talk to her father so he couldn't set up a meeting.

"Infuriating, isn't he? When he's like this he's a little boy who has lost his toy. You see what I had to put up with the last three years of my living in Denver?"

Morgan kept track of the goings-on in town, but he didn't hear a word about an angry Arthur J. Kindermann charging into Tombstone. What was he waiting for? He could follow the tire tracks of the wagon. Or could he? There would have been a lot of early morning traffic on the west road. Maybe he was still looking in empty mines out along the San Pedro River.

Morgan supervised law and order in the Silver Queen until the closing time of two A.M. There still hadn't been a word about the mine owner storming into town.

Morgan let Wally out the back door, threw the bar across the iron fittings, and headed for the guard's room. He heard a rustling behind him and whirled, his hand starting to stab for his six-gun in leather.

There was a soft laugh.

"Easy there, cowboy, with that shooting iron." Lily said. She came out of the shadows into the light of the coal oil lamp he carried.

"Wanted to thank you for helping me with my father. I was furious because you tracked me down, but that didn't last more than a minute. I decided you've done me a favor after all. I don't know what I'm going to do about going back or not going back. But at least now I have a choice.

"If I do settle down in Denver, it will not be in my father's house, but in a small house or an apartment somewhere. And I definitely want to run my own business. Not even a gambling hall, just a nice, quiet, small, high-priced, exclusive women's dress shop. Buy some in Paris and New York, and have a woman or two who will sew dresses to order. I might even design some of them.

"Now, I'm not saying I will go, but that would be what I'd want to do if I do go back."

She stood there, and he moved the light and saw

that she wore a nightgown with a robe over it.

"I was ready to go to bed, but I wanted to thank you again for helping me."

She reached up and kissed his lips. Morgan put one arm around her and set the lamp down on a poker table. He pulled her roughly to him and returned the kiss.

"How would it be if I hold you a little bit tonight. You can relax and tell me what you want to do in Denver . . . if it comes up again."

Miss Lily laughed softly. "I think we might arrange that, but let's go upstairs. My bed is bigger and softer than yours. Much better for . . . for holding each other."

Chapter Fourteen

Upstairs in Miss Lily's room, she closed the door and pushed a bolt in place, then let the robe slip off her shoulders. The nightgown she wore was so thin Morgan could see through it everywhere.

Lily stretched out on the bed and beckoned to him. Morgan sat down beside her, then lay down, and she pushed against him.

"I do want you to hold me," Lily said. "Hold me because I've got to make a decision and I'm scared, frightened half out of my head. What if it's the wrong decision?"

"Better to make one than wish you had later. Every day we make decisions. This one is just a little more dramatic than most of them."

He put his arms around her and drew her tightly against him, then kissed her cheek.

"Morgan, will you tell me true what I should do?"

"Not a chance. I only make decisions that I have to live with. You're not going to have anyone to blame if it doesn't work out, either way. Decide what would be best for Lily-Hortense, and do it. Don't worry about what other people say or think or do. You're the one who has to stare in the mirror and make peace with yourself."

She groaned. "You're not much help."

"Didn't intend to be that kind of help. Look at all of the angles, all of the benefits, the friends, the town. Is what you want the most to live your life for in Tombstone or in Denver? That should be one of the questions you ask yourself."

"Oh, damn. Kiss me, that might help." He bent, and her face turned up and the kiss lasted for a long time. Then she sighed and nibbled at his cheeks and kissed his eyes and his nose.

"If I decide to go back to Denver, will you come and live there with me?"

"No."

"Like I say, Morgan, you're no fucking help at all."

"You want to stay here and run your saloon?"

"That's better than whoring."

"True."

"So make some comment, some judgment. Oh, Morgan, you are infuriating, you know that?" She sat up, pushed away from him, and took off the see-through nightgown. It was made of fine silk.

"So here's the body that's taken on a thousand men. What do you think?"

"I think it looks good here, in your saloon. I also think it would look good in a three-thousand-dollar ball gown at some big Denver society charity event."

"Damn you, Morgan."

She began to undress him. "One thing I can't stand is a man who overdresses for the occasion. Now look at you. Definitely too many clothes on."

She took off his jacket and then his tie and his shirt.

"Now, that's better." She kissed him again, then pushed him down to her pillow and moved so one of her big breasts lowered into his mouth.

"Morgan, if you were me, what would you do?"

He bit her nipple and then pushed it away. "Sweet Hortense-Lily. I'm not you, so I don't know how to answer. I don't have a rich father, I wasn't raised in luxury in Denver, and I didn't go on the road for three years working the dance halls. I just can't tell you."

"Oh, damn!" She stood and stared down at him; then she pulled off his boots and knelt by the bed and opened his belt and his fly and pulled down his pants. She took off his underwear and then lay on top of him, her naked flesh against his.

"If you're not going to help me decide what to do, you can at least make me feel like a woman and make love to me furiously or sweet and soft, however you want to."

"I think I can agree to that," Morgan said, grinning. She kissed him, pressing her body hard against his, and in a moment he hugged her to him and rolled them both over so he was on top. He kissed her nose and watched her.

"I like the view better from up here, but we can trade off." His mouth closed over hers and the kiss was that of a lover, hot and hurried, his tongue darting into her mouth searching out her tongue and battling with it.

Lily moaned in delight and felt her body respond

to him. She ground her hips upward against him and soon felt his hardness start to form.

He found one of her breasts with his hand and held it, then gently massaged the mound, teasing her nipple, then rolling it between his finger and thumb until it rose and hardened.

"I think she likes you," Lily said, a huskiness showing in her voice. She moaned a moment later. "Oh, damn, but it's been a long time, Morgan. Too long."

She pulled his head down toward her chest, and sighed when his mouth ministered to her breasts. He nibbled on her nipples, then bit them gently and harder until she moaned and he stopped. He sucked as much of one of her breasts into his mouth as he could take, tweaking her nipple with his tongue.

Lily let out a soft wail of pleasure.

"Most of the men never cared a whit about how I felt," Lily said. "They just want to play with me a little, then slam into me and pump it off and grin and roll away and be gone. Damn, I got to hate them. I'm surprised more girls don't kill the men in whorehouses."

"Some do."

"Not enough," she said.

Lily found his manhood and grabbed it with one hand and held on. "Nothing like a good man. Always have said that. Always will. I just like men."

"Damn good thing," Morgan said. Then he trailed his kisses down from her breasts over the swell of her ribs to the hollow where her flat little belly lay. She squirmed as he went.

"Oh, Lord, Morgan. What are you doing? Oh . . . damn . . . kissing me there?"

He licked her belly button and she squealed, then he moved lower until his lips came to the soft blush of blonde hair and her mound.

Her body shivered and she lifted up to watch him. "Beautiful . . . just . . . so . . . fine!" She shivered again, and her hands rubbed his back and down as far as she could reach toward his waist.

Morgan worked over the mound with his hand, rubbing it hard, watching for her reaction, parting the soft pubic hair and driving past her soft wetness to her inner thigh. It was alabaster white, softly sleek. He kissed it once, then again, and she gasped and then wailed.

"Oh . . . marvelous . . . Morgan, I love that! No man has ever done that to me before. Wonderful. Just . . . wonderful!"

He stroked her thighs now with both his hands, working from well down almost to her crotch, but stopping before he came to the glory spot. He pushed her legs wider, and she gasped when he trailed his hand over her nether lips.

They were swollen, he could see, hot and wet and waiting for him. He brushed the lips and found just above them the small node of her clit.

Once, twice, then six times he strummed it.

Lily gasped, then shrilled a low call of surprise and wonder. "Good! Morgan . . . so . . . damn . . . fucking good."

Her body jolted into an orgasm, shaking and grinding.

"Oh, God, oh, God, oh, God!" she whispered. Then a wail came, high and loud, as her hips humped forward and her body spasmed time and time again as the sudden tremors rushed through her making her gasp for breath and suck in gulps of air as the shaking continued.

When it slowed and stopped she clutched at him.

"Oh, Christ! I haven't had an orgasm for a year! Do

you know how important this is for me?" She was still panting and gasping and shaking. She kissed him and pulled his face down and held him there in her strong arms. When she ended the kiss she still held him, and then eased up and reached for his crotch again.

"I don't know how anything could be any better. Maybe it's a sign I should get out of this damn dry hot town and go back where I belong. Maybe."

She stroked his erection until he put down a hand stopping her.

"Soon," he said.

She kissed him again, and then wrapped her legs around his back and nodded.

"Why not right now," she said. "For the first time. What do you say to about seven times tonight? You man enough to make love to me seven times before morning?"

"We'll have to start with once."

Lily shivered, panted, and then kissed him hard. "Let's start it right now before I explode!"

He moved between her satin thighs and probed and she helped and he was in.

"Oh, God! . . . how . . . oh, damn! . . . Morgan . . . Oh! Oh! Oh! That is so perfect . . . it's been too damn long!"

A moment later they both were sweating, pumping away at each other with full steam.

"Oh, Morgan! . . . so damn good!"

"Beautiful."

"Now, Morgan, faster, faster!"

Lily shrieked, and down the hallway they heard another yell of passion. Lily shrieked again and pushed him high off the soft bed and held him there a moment. Then she collapsed on the bed and Morgan kept on working.

He pulled his knees higher and poked again and again, and then it dissolved in a sheet of flames and he roared into the fire and blasted.

"Damn! Damn! Damn! Damn!" he barked. Then he too was finished, and sagged on top of Lily. Her arms came around him pinning him in place, and they panted together, resting, regaining their strength, breathing hotly against each other's shoulders.

Lily reached up and kissed his cheek. "Morgan, I don't think I can stand seven like that one."

"Lily, once when I was sixteen—" Lily hit him with a pillow, and they both grinned and rested some more.

Ten minutes later they sat side by side on the bed. Lily had uncorked her "good" Tennessee sipping whiskey and they each held a glass half full.

"I'm no farther along making my decision than I was an hour ago," Lily said. "Your fault, you made me think about other things."

"Which you hated."

"Not exactly. I've tried to figure out if it would work, my being back in Denver. I'd have to have my own place, live my own life. But would Father let me?"

"You'll have to talk to him about that. You can always go back with or without his approval."

"But I'd want him to at least be a friend, if I was in town. I guess I could even work for him, one of his departments. He has a lot of women working in his business."

"This is as close to giving you advice as I'm going to come, little lady. You could consider this a chance you might not have again, to make up with your father and go back. If it doesn't work out, you can always go back west somewhere and buy a saloon to run."

"Thanks, Morgan. I appreciate that. Now all you have to do is try to get a meeting with Father."

"That's all. First I have to figure out how I can talk to the man."

The next morning, Morgan was in the lobby of the Hanover House when the restaurant opened. He had been right. Roustenhauser was an early riser. Morgan waited until the man had ordered and was partway into his breakfast before he walked up to the man's table, pulled out a chair, and sat down.

"As of yesterday I'm not working for you anymore, Roustenhauser, so I can tell you exactly what I think of your performance. Not good."

The brewer started to rise, but Morgan put his hand out.

"Stay right there. I'm not through. Two days ago your daughter was kidnapped and held for ransom. I went after her and killed two men and brought her back safely. I've been shot at half a dozen times in this town, and when I try to set up a meeting between a father and his daughter, one of the parties acts like a two-year-old and stomps off in a fit."

Roustenhauser's face turned red and he started to rise again.

"Look, if you don't agree to a meeting with Hortense today, before noon, here in the hotel lobby, then my charges go up to a hundred dollars a day and I want my money right now. You owe me for twenty-six days. No more expense money. You have a delightful young daughter. Don't act like a fool now and destroy your relationship with her for the rest of your life."

Morgan waited for the explosion. Roustenhauser's face gradually lost its flush. The old man took a deep breath, reached for his coffee, and took a long drink. When he set the cup down it clattered in the saucer.

He scowled. "Damn," he said softly. "No man likes to admit he's wrong. I know my daughter is a grown-up woman now. I know she owns the Silver Queen. Damnit, I know how she earned her living for the past three years. I've known it for a week, but don't you tell her I know.

"Now about meeting her. Yes, I'll be here in the lobby to meet with her. I'm used to getting my own way all the time. Sometimes . . ." He stopped. "Hell, tell her I'll be glad to talk with her, and to listen to what she says. You can stay if you want to. I'll also have your money ready. Would ten o'clock be a good time?"

Morgan said it would, thanked the man, and hurried out of the hotel dining room.

A few minutes later he sat on Lily's bed and reached down and kissed her cheek. She groaned and pushed him away. She still wore nothing.

Lily awoke slowly. When she was sure she wanted to be awake, she blinked, then sat up and reached out and kissed his lips.

"You've got a date with your father, Hortense. Ten o'clock in the lobby. We had an interesting chat in the hotel dining room over coffee."

Her eyes went wide. Then she grabbed him and hugged him. "I think I need to thank you, Buckskin Lee Morgan." She stood up on the bed on her knees, her lovely body undraped.

"Just for your information, Mr. Morgan. I've decided to go back to Denver—if I can work out things with my father."

"This morning he's in a fine mood, willing to talk, and to compromise with you. My guess is he'll agree to anything you want, just to get you back in the Mile-High City."

"Yeah!" Lily yelled. "I think this is going to be a good day!"

Chapter Fifteen

Morgan left the Silver Queen, and when the stores opened he stopped by at a men's clothier on Allen Street and bought two new shirts. One of his was getting a bit frayed. He came out to the boardwalk and saw a man passing he should know. He thought back and a moment later it came to him.

The man walking the Tombstone street looking carefully at all the men he met was the guard lieutenant from the Silver Nugget mine. He was the one man at the mine who probably could identify Morgan. The guard had taken a good look at Morgan in the lantern light when the two guards stopped the wagon that night with the silver.

Morgan stayed in the store a moment longer and let him pass, then followed him a while. The guard worked every 24-hour saloon along the street. He went inside, evidently checked the players and drinkers in each one, then finally came out and watched the men on the street.

So Kindermann had found out the silver was gone and reacted. But it was not the reaction Morgan had guessed. He was taking the cautious, slow approach. The guard officer would be looking for Lenny and for the guy riding the wagon with him.

Not a large problem for Morgan. He would not be overly public for a day or two.

He waited until the guard had passed by the Silver Queen because it wasn't open. Then Morgan went in with a knock on the door.

Lily danced down the stairs. She was in a dress not quite so conservative, but still not revealing. She twirled around and grinned at him.

"How do I look?"

"Beautiful, cautious, a little scared, which is good, and maybe even a little contrite. Ready to put your best side forward and make peace with your father."

She came to him slowly, then kissed his cheek and hugged him. "Morgan, that about describes me right now. Unsure, a little bit plain scared, but knowing now that I want to go back to Denver and be friends with my father. I'm really going to try. I think my rebellion is over, and I'm more grown-up now. Not a snotty kid anymore. At least I hope."

"Good sign. How much time do we have?"

Lily grinned. "Not near enough time for that."

"I was thinking of a cup of coffee."

They went back to the dining room and found a pot of boiled coffee still on the back of the kitchen stove.

"Any regrets?" he asked.

"Sure, a few. But a lot more excitement. I'm going to open a women's shop in Denver. There are a few, but mine will be the best, the nicest, plush, luxurious. I want to appeal to all the rich women in Denver, and there are a lot of them."

"What if your father doesn't want you to do that?"

"Then I'll work on him gradually, show him that I have the experience and the business sense to make a go of it. Also I'll show him that I'm using my own money, and won't expect any backing from him."

"Sounds like a good solid, intelligent, grown-up approach to dealing with your father." Morgan looked at his pocket watch. "We just about have time to walk over there to the hotel and not be late. Now, don't be nervous, be your new cautious, honest self."

They started for the hotel. He told her about the guard officer from the mine in town staring at every man he met.

"So if I suddenly vanish from your side, you'll know why. I'm not sure that he would remember my face, but he just might. That must be Kindermann's approach, slow and cautious."

"How long until the investors from Phoenix can get here?" she asked.

"Another four days. Don't worry. If he sees me I'll reason with him. Probably with the end of my .45. But it will be fine."

They got to the hotel without Morgan spotting the guard, who was now wearing a new tan hat with a low crown and denim pants and shirt and no vest.

Morgan walked Lily up the front steps of the hotel and got some stares. They went to the side of the lobby where Roustenhauser sat reading a newspaper. He put it down and stood at once.

"Ah, Hortense, good, and Mr. Morgan."

He handed Morgan an envelope. "Thanks again for being so honest with me this morning. I believe this will cover our contractual arrangements."

"I'm sure it will. I'm going to leave you alone now. I hope everything works out all right."

Morgan turned and walked away feeling good about the meeting. The room clerk called to him and he went that way.

"Two messages for you, Mr. Morgan. I missed you this morning."

One was in an envelope with postage on it. He opened it first and found it was from Delsey. He leaned against the wall near the front door and read it.

"Mr. Morgan. I made it to Phoenix and found my aunt and I'm staying here and helping out at the store. It's a beautiful store and my aunt is a marvel. I'm learning so much. I want to thank you again for helping me. I owe my life to you, and if you come north this way, be sure to stop in Phoenix and see me. I want to show you my gratitude again.

"I hope to see you one of these days."

It was signed by Delsey and gave her address and the address and name of the jewelry store. Morgan smiled and folded the letter in its envelope and put it in his pocket.

The other note was from the chief of police. Chief Inman asked Morgan to stop by his office at his convenience. Now seemed like a good time.

On the way to the chief's office, Morgan watched the street. He saw the guard officer coming out of a saloon on the other side of the street. The man paused, then turned and went along the far side of Allen Street watching the men. Soon he vanished into another saloon.

Chief Inman looked up when Morgan came in. He nodded and pointed to his private office. Inside the room, the chief shut the door and waved to a chair.

"Makes me mad what that asshole Potts did to you. Hell, any lawman worth his badge can figure out you got hog-tied by an angry relative. Now I want to help you out."

"Appreciate that, Chief. But there's no way to call in those damn wanted posters once they've been mailed out."

"True, but I figured I can do the next best thing. I talked to the current sheriff, Dirkin. He's shit-scared of Potts. Won't do a damn thing about that wanted.

"So I'll do the next best thing. I'll send out a flyer to every lawman in the West, explaining that the old wanted is no good, that the death took place in my jurisdiction, not the sheriff's, and that it was purely a matter of self-defense. I'll ask any lawmen who have that wanted to burn it at once and keep a notice on file that it is invalid and won't be paid on."

Morgan nodded and grinned. "Best possible action I could have hoped for, Chief," he said. "Course there will always be a few of them still out there, but I can live with that. I've made it through the past four years and haven't been shot at more than a couple of dozen times."

"Sorry Tombstone did this to you, Morgan. You seem like a right regular kind of a man. Anyplace you have trouble with that wanted, you tell the sheriff or police chief to send me a letter. I'll straighten them out in a rush."

Morgan got up and shook the chief's hand. "Appreciate it, Chief."

Morgan left with a lift to his step. At least he had one friend in Tombstone instead of a blood-feud enemy. Morgan wasn't watching the street as he came out of the police office. He nearly ran into a man, and too late saw that he was the guard from the Silver Nugget mine.

The man looked at him, snorted, and backed off a step, his hand near his six-gun.

"Yeah, you're the one," the guard said. "I got a

man down at the saddle shop who wants to see you. Don't know your name, but I remember that face. Need to talk to you about a heavy load you hauled out of the Silver Nugget a couple of nights ago."

Morgan's right hand fluttered a moment near his Colt .45. "Not sure what you're talking about, stranger. But if that hand of yours comes any closer to iron, you better be reaching for it fast. I don't like people ordering me around."

"Then you won't come peaceable?"

"You've got a hog-leg, draw it instead of crowing."

The guard hesitated. "Some folks think I've got a good draw. You sure you want to find out?"

"Do it!" Morgan shouted. The man's hand darted for his gun, but before he had it out of leather, Morgan's Colt belched smoke and a .45-caliber chunk of lead slammed into the guard's right shoulder. It jolted him backwards three feet and sprawled him on his back. His weapon fell out of the leather and Morgan stepped up and kicked the iron away.

The guard held his shoulder and blood seeped between his fingers.

"Bastard!" the guard bellowed.

"You started the draw first, tenderfoot. I finished my draw faster. Tell your friend if he wants to talk to me, he has to send a better man than you."

A man knelt beside the guard, helped him stand, and led him down the street toward Dr. Schroder's office.

Morgan frowned at the little knot of people that had gathered to watch. His expression sent most of them on their way. He went across the street and leaned against a post on an overhang for a while until those still watching gave up and moved on. Then Morgan walked with a purpose toward the saddle shop. He had never seen Kindermann. Now might be a good time to identify him. Morgan knew he was going to need to know who Kindermann was sooner or later.

Morgan reached the saddle shop and went inside. The wonderful smell of the raw leather came to him and he paused a moment just sniffing. Two men were in the place, one with a knife working on a piece of leather. The other one must be the customer. He was an inch over six feet, with thick blond hair starting to gray and a full well-trimmed beard about the same shade of blondish gray. So he was Kindermann.

Morgan looked at some hand-tooled belts, passed them, and ran his hand over a newly crafted saddle. It was a good job. Had decorations of pounded silver. Worth a year's wages.

"Yes, sir, Mr. Kindermann. I'm working on your new saddle. It should be done in about two weeks." The leather man looked up and saw Morgan. "Morning, something I can do for you, sir?" the leather man asked.

Morgan shook his head. "Just dreaming about this saddle. What's it worth?"

"Not sure about the worth, but my price on it is a hundred and twenty dollars."

"Figures. It's worth it. Beautiful piece of work."

"Thanks."

Morgan waved, looked at Kindermann once more, and walked out of the shop. Back at the Silver Queen Saloon, Wally was getting ready to open up at noon. It was past eleven o'clock.

"Miss Lily isn't back yet?" Morgan asked.

Wally shook his head. "Must be something important."

"It is, Wally. I better get over there and check."

When Morgan arrived at the hotel lobby, Mr. Roustenhauser had just given Lily a hand to help her up. She was smiling, and so was her father.

Morgan came up and waited until they saw him.

"Morgan, we were about to have a celebration, a dinner. I'm moving back to Denver as soon as I can wind up my affairs here—in a month or so, I expect."

Her father smiled. "She's going to go into the women's clothes business. I think she'll do well. All of our friends will soon be customers."

"Sounds like it was a good talk. But you two have your celebration. I'm still wondering about a man I saw this morning."

Lily winked and grinned and took her father's arm and walked with him into the dining room. Not an eye was raised.

Morgan went back to the street, eyed the boardwalk both ways, then strode across the dirt street avoiding the horse droppings and their colonies of buzzing flies.

He had just taken a step up to the curb when he saw two men waiting for him. Morgan's shot-up left shoulder still pained him and he wasn't ready for a fistfight. They were too close for him to draw.

They looked at him again, shook their heads, and walked on up the street.

"Thought you were a friend of ours," one of them said as they passed.

Morgan drew in a deep breath and walked on down to the Silver Queen. It was open for business, and he pulled his hat well down over his eyes and sat down at his post in the back. He didn't have to be there, but he figured he'd be hiding if he went into his guard's room.

Was the silver still there? He waited a half hour, then went to the room and checked. It was there, exactly where he had left it. He pushed the blanket back around the silver bars and wandered out to the kitchen. One of the girls was the cook. She had just finished a stew and ladled him out some. It was good.

Morgan knew he wasn't needed in the saloon until after supper. It was a haven. But he didn't need any damn haven. He finished the stew, thanked the girl, and went to the street. He walked down half a dozen stores and looked in the hardware window at a new Winchester shotgun.

He felt someone come up behind him, and before he could turn around a six-gun muzzle poked hard into his ribs.

"You turn slow and easy or you're one dead piece of cowboy. Turn now and let me get a better look at you."

Morgan turned slowly, his hands low along his legs. When Morgan came around, he saw that the gunman was the guard from the Silver Nugget Mine. His right shoulder was bandaged and his arm inside his shirt in a makeshift sling. The gun wavered in the man's left hand.

"That's one way to outdraw a man," Morgan said. "Just what the hell do you think you're going to do next?"

Chapter Sixteen

The guard officer from the Silver Nugget Mine looked at Morgan with puzzlement. "What am I going to do next? Simple. I'm going to take you to see Mr. Kindermann. He's staying at the hotel tonight."

"Here we are in plain sight on the main street of Tombstone with a hundred people within my shouting distance and you think you can pull a gun on me and march me off?"

"Exactly what I'm doing right now."

"Even though you hold that six-gun in your left hand, you've never fired it left-handed, and right now your hand is shaking so hard you can barely hold the weapon."

"What do you mean?" The man looked down at his .44, and Morgan's right hand moved so quickly the gunman never saw it. Morgan's doubled-up fist smashed into the bony side of the man's wrist and jolted it downward, spilling the six-gun from his grasp. Morgan's other hand slammed against the shot-up shoulder, and the guard screeched in pain as he dropped to his knees.

Morgan kicked the six-gun to one side, then brought his knee up into the gunman's chin, snapping his head backward and knocking him unconscious on the boardwalk in front of a lawyer's office. After staring at the man for a moment, Morgan turned and walked down the boardwalk and into a land sales firm. He went through it, out the back, up the alley, and into the Silver Queen Saloon's rear door.

He remembered the pair of new shirts. Now he changed clothes, putting on one of the fancy shirts, then a string tie, and a black hat with a flat brim, which he settled on his head.

It gave him a different look and he wouldn't be that easy for the angry guard to spot in a crowd.

Kindermann interested Morgan more than the guard. He went out the front door of the saloon and across the street to the Hanover House. A quick look at the register while the room clerk was busy showed Morgan that Kindermann had Rooms 22 and 23. Probably one for him and one for the guard who now had a shot-up shoulder, a sore left wrist, and a jaw that would creak and groan every time he took a bite for the next year.

Morgan waited for an hour in the lobby, but Kindermann didn't make an appearance. Could he be in his room? Morgan went up the stairs to the second floor and saw no one in the short hallway. He knocked on the door of Room 23, but nobody answered. He could hear no movement inside through the door. Morgan used his set of three skeleton keys. The second one opened the simple keyhole lock.

He edged the door inward until he could see that no one was there. Quickly he checked the room. One small bag, no suitcase, no clothes in the closet, a quick overnight trip.

He could wait for the mine owner to come back. Wait. Why was Kindermann staying in the hotel when he had a house in town, a mansion really? It didn't make sense. Unless this was a trap. He stepped to the door and cracked it and looked out.

Two men stood down the hall in one direction. Both of them had shotguns. He looked in the other direction. One man stood there talking with another who was Kindermann. Morgan was boxed in. He locked the door, pushed the straight-backed chair under the door knob to brace it closed, and then hurried to the window.

The frame pushed up easily, and Morgan looked out. He was on the second floor in back and there was only a narrow ledge outside the window, maybe eight inches wide. Below that lay the hard-packed ground of the alley. He needed a rope.

A key turned in the door lock, and Morgan had no choice. He pushed through the window and placed his feet firmly on the ledge. He moved toward Room 24 and he hoped that no one was in it.

His first instinct had been to face the wall, but he knew it would be better with his back against the wall. He took a slow step sideways and pushed himself over in that direction, his back brushing along the shiplap of the wall. He took two more small steps and then heard the pounding on the door of Room 23. A moment later a shotgun blast echoed through the building and the door splintered.

He moved again and again. Then his hand

touched the window frame. There was no time to open the window. He fisted his hand and hit the window glass in the center. The glass shattered inward and he felt a cut on his hand.

With his arm, he smashed the rest of the glass out of the middle of the window and stepped in, then pulled the rest of his body past the jagged glass. There was no one in the room.

Just as he vanished inside the room, a head pushed out the window of Room 23 and looked up and down outside.

"Must have dropped to the ground," Kindermann said. "Get down there and cover both ends of the alley. Move. Run, dammit!"

Morgan listened out the window, then went to the door and saw that it was unlocked. He eased it open a half inch and looked out. Two men with shotguns ran down the far stairs. A moment later another man came in his direction and flashed past heading for the near stairway.

Morgan waited. They couldn't check every room on the floor, but they might be smart enough to check those on each side of where he had been. That meant move. He opened the door, went out, closed it gently, then walked down to Room 29, his room, and unlocked it and stepped inside.

He was now two doors from the stairs and five away from where he had been. The hallway was quiet for a moment. Then Kindermann came out and paced it for a while, then went back in the room and came out again.

One of the shotgunners ran up the stairs and reported to the boss. It wasn't good news. Kindermann did some shouting and ordered the man to leave.

What better time than right now for a heart-to-heart talk with Kindermann? Morgan checked his six-gun and waited what he figured was time enough for Kindermann to do some tall thinking. Then Morgan slipped out of his room and hurried down to the one Kindermann had entered.

He wondered about the lock and his key, but when he got there he backed to the hall wall, lifted his good right foot, and kicked against the door just beside the knob. The locking bolt slipped past the facing plate and the door slammed open.

"What in the—"

Morgan's six-gun covered Kindermann. Morgan closed the door behind him and locked it again.

"Afternoon, Mr. Kindermann. Evidently you were looking for me, so I figured I'd come and find out what you wanted."

Kindermann had shown fear when Morgan first came in, but he controlled it quickly and now stared in defiance at him.

"You. You're this Morgan person. My man said you were with Lenny the night he stole some of my property."

"Why be so delicate, Kindermann? I hear that Lenny only took what he considered his fair share of the silver that you stole from the owners of the mine, the real owners, the stockholders who own seventy-five percent of the stock in the Silver Nugget."

"How in hell . . . That's not true. I own the mine. What I do with my own silver is my business."

"As a liar, you're not much good, Kindermann, even though you must get a lot of practice. Three names for you. Ambrose S. White, Joseph G. Johnson, and Warren G. Bellevue. Do those names strike a responsive chord in that black heart of yours?"

"Doesn't matter. You evidently know what Lenny did with the silver. He must have left it in town, since my men have assured me that Lenny bought a horse and rode out of Tombstone early that same morning the silver was stolen."

"Your men don't know what they're talking about. That man who rode out was a drifter Lenny hired. He told me it would confuse you and make you go wild. How was your series of tours of the closed mines and tunnels in the area? It must have been tough work."

"You bastard!" Kindermann exploded. "You know a lot more about this than you're telling me."

"Lenny said you stole about twenty percent of the output of the Silver Nugget and gave him fifty dollars every time he helped you. How much silver are you missing, about a ton?"

"You dirty bastard."

"What I'm more interested in are the three tally men before Lenny. Each of them wound up dead. I know, I know, I can't prove it. But you see, that's the beauty of my system. Right here in my hand I have the sheriff, the judge, the jury, and the executioner. This court doesn't take much proof. I'm just as sure that you killed the wives of two of those men as well."

"You're babbling, Morgan. Out of your mind. Why would I do any of that?"

"To shut up the tally men, and get back the money you were holding for them. Then the other reason was to get the young, attractive wives of those men in your bed. You're a cockhound, everyone knows it."

Kindermann's face flushed and he turned and lunged at Morgan, but the deadly muzzle of the Colt .45 stopped him.

"You ready to die right here, Kindermann? If you are, take one more step toward me and I'll blow your murdering brains out!"

Kindermann faded back and sat on the bed.

"Things went your way for too long, Kindermann. You used to be a good hard-rock miner and a mine operator. Then you got greedy. That will usually do it in the best of men." Morgan motioned with the iron.

"Get up. I've changed my mind. This town deserves to know what a murdering bastard you are. Get up. You and I are going for a walk down to Chief Inman's office where you're going into a jail cell. We'll be able to find plenty of men to testify against you. Tombstone will revel in spitting on you during the trial, then get to see you shit your pants just before the trap drops as you're hung."

Kindermann wiped sweat from his forehead. "I'm not moving from this bed."

Morgan shrugged and cocked the deadly .45. "Fine with me," he said, and shot the mine owner in the thigh.

The roaring sound of the revolver going off inside the room was deafening for a minute. Then Kindermann's screams came through. The slug had sliced through the meaty part of his thigh and exited into the bed covers.

Kindermann had slammed back on the bed and wailed and keened in agony.

Morgan stood over him and cocked the weapon again.

"I figure I can shoot you ten to twelve times before I hit something vital. You could live another hour, maybe two. Now do you believe I'll do what I say I'll do?"

Kindermann nodded. "Tie up my leg and I'll go to the police office."

Morgan wouldn't help the man walk. A few minutes later they went down the back stairs of the hotel, into the alley, and down to the street and along toward the city police office.

A man shouted from across the street. "Mr. Kindermann, you been hurt?" The man ran across the street and two more came with him.

Kindermann dropped to his knees. "Kill this bastard. He's Morgan. He shot me for no reason."

Morgan saw the men grab for guns. There were 20 people in the area and he decided not to confront the three gunmen there. He ran directly to the rear, right into the general store. There Morgan sprinted to the back of the establishment and out the door. Then he surveyed the alley, picked his spot behind a heavy wooden packing box, and waited.

All three men came boiling out at the same time. He put down the first with a shot to the chest, and nicked the second one in the leg before he and the third found protection.

"You men willing to die for a rat like Kindermann?" Morgan called. The heavy wooden box absorbed two rounds of fire.

"You know he killed Taft Tambert, the jasper who was the tally man in the reduction building before Lenny took over. Kindermann killed him so he couldn't tell how Kindermann was stealing the stockholders of half of their silver."

"Not true," one of the men shouted.

"Go ask him. He's killed at least three tally men and two of their wives. He's a butchering cockhound who doesn't deserve your help or your loyalty."

The two men didn't fire anymore.

"How is your friend?" Morgan asked.

"Looks like he's hit bad," one of the men said.

"If you want to pick him up and get him to the doctor, I won't fire at you."

"Honest?"

"Kindermann is the rat around here, not me. Go get your friend, you might be able to save his life."

The two men came out from their hiding spots cautiously. Then when they didn't take any fire, they holstered their weapons and picked up the shot man and carried him back through the general store.

Morgan scowled. He'd decided not to execute the damned killer in the hotel, and now Kindermann had slipped away because of a chance meeting on the street. Next time the alley. If there was a next time.

Now Kindermann would come after him with every gunman he could hire. In a town like Tombstone he should be able to round up 20 shooters in a couple of hours.

That meant Morgan had to pick the time and the place. He'd make it as hard as possible. An idea started to form in his mind. Soon Morgan was grinning. He hurried down the alley, into the next alley, and ran into the back door of the Silver Queen.

He found what he wanted in Lily's room upstairs and began working on it on his knees in the whorehouse hallway.

Chapter Seventeen

Two of the girls came up and looked at what Morgan was doing. He had a pen and an ink pot and a three-foot-square piece of white cardboard. On it he wrote a message in two-inch-high letters. It said:

"KINDERMANN. I'm ready to meet you. Come alone to the San Pedro River where the first branch creek runs into it north of the west trail. I'll be there at ten A.M. tomorrow. Don't be late. We'll settle this problem once and for all." Morgan signed the notice, then went and put it up on the big community bulletin board that the general store on Allen Street prided itself on.

Anything important happening in town showed up first on the bulletin board. The proprietor of the store cleaned it off once or twice a week, but it had better readership than either of the two local newspapers.

It was nearly three o'clock when Morgan got the sign posted. Plenty of time for Kindermann to see it. Just to make sure, Morgan wrote a note:

"Mr. Kindermann. There's a message for you on the bulletin board. You better see what it says." Morgan put the note in an envelope and hired a small boy to take it Kindermann, either at the doctor's office or the hotel.

Back at the saloon, Lily was there starting to tally up things. She wanted to know what she had on hand when she sold the place.

She took time out to thank Morgan for getting her father in such a good mood.

"I don't know when I've seen him so pleased, so comfortable, not yelling, listening to what I said, going along with my plans to live in a house of my own and to start my own business. Wow! Talk about turning my life around in twenty-four hours."

"Who you going to sell to?"

"Who? I've had half a dozen men trying to buy me out. I've narrowed it down to two of them. They are supposed to give me their bids this afternoon. Then I pick out the one I want, bargain him up a few thousand, and close the deal."

"How much?"

"I bet twenty thousand for the Queen in that poker game."

"But this is no poker game."

"True. I'll be lucky to get eighteen. The property and the building are mine, so that helps."

"Oh, just a reminder, what's under the bed doesn't go with the Silver Queen," Morgan said.

Later, over supper, he told her about his talk with Kindermann.

"You went right into his hotel room and waited for him?"

"My mistake. But we had a good chat."

"So he knows that his partners in Phoenix are coming. He'll want to steal what he can and run before they get here."

"That's why I'm sure he'll show up tomorrow. I had to make the spot far enough out of town so we wouldn't have a couple of thousand spectators."

"You know he'll bring a bunch of guns out there to get you," Lily said.

"He'll try."

"When are you going out there?"

"About three o'clock this morning. I want to make some improvements. It's a natural little fortress I've picked out. But some small additions will help. Reminds me. I need to get over to the hardware store before he closes."

Morgan went in the back door just before the hardware man closed. He bought a pound of large-headed roofing nails an inch and a half long. The hardware man raised his brows when Morgan paid him.

"I suppose this has something to do with your notice on the bulletin board," the hardware man said.

"I guess you can suppose anything you want to. There isn't any law against buying roofing nails, is there?"

"Not a one, Mr. Morgan. Not a one."

Morgan left by the back door, and spent the next hour in his room working over his purchase.

He laid out the remaining sticks and half sticks of dynamite he had left from what he had bought before. The new-fangled explosive was handy, and could be used in so many ways that black powder couldn't.

He counted out 16 half sticks and put them carefully on the bed. He took the roofing nails with their big flat heads and spread them out.

Carefully Morgan wrapped the roofing nails around the half sticks of dynamite, binding them in place with sticky tape. He put ten of the roofing nails on each of the half sticks and left room for a detonator to be pushed in.

When he had half of the sticks taped up with nails, he opened the box of detonators. He used a wooden pencil to make a hole in a stick of dynamite and pushed the closed end of the detonator into the powder. The hollow end received a piece of burning fuse. He cut each strip of fuse six inches long.

Most fuse burned a foot a minute, so a six-inch fuse could burn up to 30 seconds. Most fuse burned faster than that, though. If he needed to he could cut the fuses to half that length when he was using them.

He taped the 20 half sticks he had left in bundles of four, to make two-stick explosions, and fused them the same way but without the nails.

He'd seen small bombs made that way before. When the dynamite exploded it would send those roofing nails spraying out like grapeshot, and would kill anything they hit in the right place. With enough of them he could wipe out an infantry company before the men knew what hit them.

Lily was busy getting an inventory ready, so he left her to her work and slipped out of the alley door and went to the livery stable. There he rented a different horse than he had used before, and saddled and tied the mare up behind the saloon. He checked on her twice, and about ten o'clock lay down in his room for a few hours of sleep.

He had mastered the trick of waking up whenever

he needed to, and this time he instructed his mind to awaken him at three A.M.

The trip out to the river in the blue-blackness of three A.M. took him an hour. He found the spot he wanted. He had noticed it when he was out there before to find Miss Lily. It looked even better at night, but the light of day would show some problems. He guessed that Kindermann would have his men out there by daylight digging in, finding cover, and setting up firing lanes. It wouldn't help them a damn bit.

What Morgan had found was a rocky cliff, an upthrust of tough granite that had outlasted the rest of the surrounding terrain and had not worn down through the ages.

It soared a hundred feet from the rest of the slopes and low hills, and where it came to the desert landscape, it had developed a cleft, an opening no more than two feet wide at the front that widened back ten or 12 feet to the rest of the upthrust granite wall.

The whole thing had a slight overhang, so no one could get above and drop in rocks or bombs. When Morgan got there, he rode south a half mile and tied his horse to a weathered bit of greasewood, then carried his gunny sack and ran back to the slanting cliff.

He climbed up about 50 feet from the river to the cleft and checked it to be sure. Even in the dark he was surprised how good it was. There were chunks of rock and slabs that had fallen off probably when water seeped into cracks and then froze and expanded and acted like a wedge to break off the chunk.

His first job was to pile up these slabs and chunks

to fill in the two-foot void. As he did it, he left firing slots. He had brought two repeating rifles with him, both Spencers since they could be reloaded so quickly. They had seven shots in a tube in the stock that fed the .52-caliber rounds into the firing chamber. He had 12 tubes each loaded with seven rounds, plus another hundred loose rounds in a box.

Taking out one empty tube from the butt plate and putting in a loaded one could be accomplished in about ten seconds. He worked until he had the opening closed up with a stack of rocks more than six feet high. He had four firing slots through the rocks, each wide enough so he could angle his weapon from side to side and up and down.

The holes were not so big that they would be easy to fire through from the outside even with a rifle.

On the left side of the firing slots he put a flat slab of rock, standing up about three feet off the ground and supported by other slabs of flat rocks. On this he placed one of the rifles, his six-gun and his extra rounds, and his sack of dynamite bombs. He had a packet of stinker matches ready to use on the fuses.

He took out the rest of his supplies from the gunny sack. They included a loaf of fresh-baked bread, a half pound of cheddar cheese, and two canteens of water.

Morgan was ready. He ate from the bread and cheese and then had a long drink. Then he settled down against the rocks and took the luxury of a nap. It was not quite five o'clock when he dozed off. He would be awake at daylight in an hour.

When daylight came, Morgan roused and looked out through his firing slots. He expected to see someone coming down the trail from town. There were dozens on the road, most of them miners on their way to the tunnels both upstream and downstream from the spot where the road hit the river.

Morgan watched them, and soon discovered half a dozen who had stopped along the road and stared around. One man on a bay soon came along and ordered the men to one side and then began positioning them in hidden positions. He seemed to be using the place where the road came the closest to the San Pedro River as the focal point.

Morgan watched. An hour later the miners going to work had all passed and Morgan could see only about half the men he knew had been hidden out there.

Morgan lit a match and watched the smoke from it. A slight movement of air through the cracks in his wall in the slot carried the smoke almost straight upward along the face of the rock. With any luck the blue smoke from his rifle shots would go the same way and that could mask his position for a while.

About nine o'clock, he saw a new horseman arrive. He couldn't be certain, but it seemed that the man who had positioned the others rode up to the new arrival and they talked. A minute later the man who had positioned the others rode away and hid his horse. The other horses had been taken upstream and around a small bend in the river.

Morgan watched the new man on the horse and was sure he was Kindermann. Morgan could stop it right then by putting a slug through Kindermann's chest. He was little more than 75 yards away. It was like shooting fish in a pond.

He sighted in with the Spencer, then shifted his sighting and fired one round. The big lead slug took the dun Kindermann rode in the side of its head just in back of its eye and the animal and rider went down.

Kindermann cowered behind the horse. It was the best cover for 20 yards.

Morgan pulled the rifle back inside the rocks and watched the blue-tinged smoke lift lazily toward the face of the cliff and drift upward, thinning out as it went. He doubted if the men out front could see it.

"Morgan, you bastard," Kindermann bellowed. "Show yourself. Let's get this over with. Man to man, you and me with pistols. My men won't fire."

Morgan didn't take the bait. The lieutenant came running back and heroically made it to the mine owner's side behind his dead horse. They both looked over the horse at the cliff.

Suddenly four rounds slammed into the rocks of the cliff, and one hit the new wall blocking the entrance.

Morgan looked through the lowest shooting slot. He decided the dance should begin. He set the second Spencer beside the lowest firing slot and crouched and pushed the other one through. He had targeted four men to the left side who had the least cover from his position.

He fired two shots at each of the four men. He hit two of them and sent the other two bellowing in rage and running to the rear and better protection.

He grabbed the second rifle and fired twice into the dead horse covering Kindermann, then waited for someone to move. Two men below and to the left lifted up and charged the wall. Morgan brought down one of them and the other one turned, with slugs kicking up dust all around him.

Calmly Morgan reloaded the first Spencer and watched.

"We know where you are now, Morgan. You're buzzard bait."

"Then come and get me, Kindermann. It's

twenty-five to one."

Two more men rushed forward and Morgan cut down one. Then the mine owner got smart and sent everyone charging toward Morgan at once. Morgan couldn't shoot all of them. He waited until they were close to the wall, barely 30 feet away, and then he cut the fuses in half on four of his roofing nail bombs and lit and threw them one after the other, dropping them among the 15 men who had gotten close to the cliff.

The first bomb went off to shocked silence, followed by the shrill screams of the wounded. Then the other three exploded in a deadly walking pattern along the front of the cliff. Morgan heard some of the nails zinging against the rock walls above and beside him.

When he looked out a firing slot he saw half of the men below wounded and bleeding and unable to move. Two more lifted up and ran to the rear, evidently unhurt. Three more men sat up screaming in pain.

Morgan watched the others who had been too far back to get hit by the dynamite grenades. One by one they lifted up and darted to the rear. Morgan let them go. He fired twice more into the dead horse and once just over the top of it, but found no human flesh.

For a moment it was desert quiet. Morgan could hear a shrill argument before the wails of the injured men came again.

He saw movement, and then the lieutenant behind the dead horse jumped up and ran to the rear. There was a pistol shot and the lieutenant staggered and fell. Morgan put three more rounds into the dead horse.

Morgan figured it was time to leave. He put the

extra ammunition and cheese in the gunny sack, added the dynamite bombs, and holstered his six-gun. He slung one of the Spencers and carried the other one with seven rounds in the magazine and one in the chamber.

Morgan climbed his six-foot wall in the slot of the cliff, looked down at the wounded men, and warned them with his rifle not to fire. Then he jumped down to the outside and ran down through the wounded and toward the mine owner still behind his horse.

When Morgan got halfway there he realized he was near to pistol range and he circled to the right, keeping the Spencer ready.

He saw Kindermann crawling away. He was ten feet from the horse now, not looking behind.

Morgan was aware of men leaving the area behind him. Some of the wounded who could walk had dropped their weapons and moved toward their horses.

He had closed to within 30 feet of Kindermann when he sensed someone coming. He turned and saw a man on a horse galloping straight at Kindermann. The man had blood on both sleeves of his shirt and his face. He spurred his horse and drove straight at the man on the ground.

Kindermann looked up at the last minute and saw his own hired shooter aiming a six-gun at him. The revolver went off four times. Three of the rounds hit Kindermann. Then the horse was on him and the sharp hooves sliced through the dying flesh before the horse was gone.

Morgan took one last look at the earthly remains of one Arthur J. Kindermann. At last the man had gotten what he deserved. Morgan turned and trotted downstream where he had hidden his horse.

* * *

Three days later the six partners in the Silver Nugget Mine arrived in Tombstone. Morgan met the stage and told them what he had seen and what he knew to have taken place. He turned over a wagon to the men that was loaded with 90 silver bars, and they fell all over him telling him how honest he was and how they appreciated it.

He told them he had kept two of the bars for himself and two of them for the widow of the last man Kindermann had killed in the mine. They said they understood, and took charge of the wagon and hurried out to the mine.

Morgan had one last night with Lily.

About midnight she tickled his chin and snuggled against him.

"The saloon sale went through today. A lawyer drew up the papers and I got my twenty-one thousand in cash. I've put it in the bank here, and the bank owner will send a bank draft for that amount to my bank in Denver. It's worked before.

"Oh, I've decided that I'm going to keep my Lily name. I always hated Hortense as a name anyway. I'll be Lily Roustenhauser." She put her hand down to excite him again.

"Morgan, where are you heading next?"

"Phoenix. I have some silver to deliver. Then I've been thinking of going to the coast again. Been a while."

"The new man came to manage the Silver Nugget today. The stockholders figure that Kindermann stole over a hundred and fifty thousand dollars worth of silver over the past three years. Most of it is in another unused tunnel out at the mine. He had forty thousand in the local bank which the partners were awarded.

"They promised that from now on one of them

will be living in Tombstone full time, and the Silver Nugget will treat its workers right."

"Shut up," Morgan said softly. "Give me something to remember on that long ride to Phoenix."

Lily did, and Morgan smiled every mile until the stage reached Phoenix and he could deliver the 40 pounds of silver to Delsey Tambert.